BLINK IF YOU LOVE ME

Blink If You Love Me

A novel
by

DAVID MOSCOVICH

Adelaide Books
New York / Lisbon
2019

BLINK IF YOU LOVE ME
A novel
By David Moscovich

Published by Adelaide Books, New York / Lisbon
adelaidebooks.org

Editor-in-Chief
Stevan V. Nikolic

For any information, please address Adelaide Books
at info@adelaidebooks.org
or write to:
Adelaide Books
244 Fifth Ave. Suite D27
New York, NY, 10001

ISBN-10: 1-950437-29-9
ISBN-13: 978-1-950437-29-0

Printed in the United States of America

Dedicated, with gratitude, to Lydia Davis

Oh nothingness, I have to have visions,

I can't have visions, I have to love:

I have to be wrong to write.

— Kathy Acker (from Don Quixote)

This is a work of fiction.

Contents

Journal #1 (red)

Journal #3 (green)

June 3

The Case of the Panty-Kisser

Eva had been experiencing a rash around her crotch for some time and suspected that the origin had something to do with her panties, but this was a great day – a day in which this long-standing mystery would be solved.

Eva walked into the closet behind the kitchen – this is a tucked away space which contains the laundry machine and a drying rack suspended above an industrial-style sink where she likes to hang her panties. I admit that I have helped Eva squeeze these panties with a method performed by my grandmother – as a child, I had watched her old-world forearms gain muscle tissue as she wrung out laundry to hang on the clothesline. Here, the cleaning lady, C, was not supposed to meddle – Eva would always leave notes written on lined paper stating that nobody should mix or move the panties hanging there to dry.

It is one phrase I have memorized: *não mexer*. Therefore, what did Eva see when she went to check on her underwear the morning in question?

C, the cleaning lady, standing on her tip toes, pressing the panties to her cheek and right over her fleshy lips, because lips are the most sensitive skin with which to test the wetness.

This one is still a little damp, C whispers to herself, kissing the next, and the next, right smack on the most intimate pocket at the very center of the panties.

I imagine a wide range of emotion occurs when seeing the cleaning lady press one's undergarments flush against her lips – contemplative, alone at the drying rack – testing for moisture.

June 5

When To Poo

This was one conversation I had hoped to avoid having with my brother-in-law, A, within earshot of his mother, within whispering distance of my father-in-law, Big A – but after my wife announced to the entire household that I was on the verge of intestinal rupture, A. came downstairs to discuss the timing and particularities of my near future digestive drift.

I had assumed these types of details would remain private – a murmur of discussion between Eva and myself, never to leave the sanctity and intimacy of husband and wife's insider information. But this is not the way of Eva's household.

I am about to clean the bathroom, said her brother A, so why don't you go first. You're going #2, correct?

No, that's okay, I said, you go ahead and clean.

My face was flushed with shame – no adult outside of my own parents had ever used the term #2 with me – not in its imminent, pragmatic sense – and my own mom and dad hadn't since I was about two feet tall.

No, really, he said, you should go now because there's no point in my cleaning if you will just make a mess afterwards. And, he added, be quick.

This was one conversation I had really hoped to avoid.

Not only was my wife's brother asking me to go #2 – which in itself was surreal – but he was asking me to do it quickly, under a time limit. Was he going to stand outside the bathroom door with a stopwatch? There was no way I could perform under these conditions. I blushed, feeling infantilized, humiliated. I had the distinct feeling that I had ceased to be a man.

When the cleaning was finished and the subject matter seemed to have been forgotten, I entered the bathroom to do my business.

Eva knocked and opened the door simultaneously, and delivered me her lips while I was on the throne.

Give me a kiss, she said, and pressed into me.

The Cleaning Lady and the Hair Dryer

Everyone is coughing in the house – Big A is sick and shuttling through the medicine bag in the kitchen for relief. Eva's mom is making a tea. Eva's brother is asleep, upstairs.

C, the cleaning lady, offers her advice:

When my nose is running, I just plug in the hair dryer and point it towards my nose so it dries everything all the way to my throat.

I look at Eva. Eva looks at Big A — an imposing figure, tallest of the family, with broad shoulders and a thick black beard.

Eva's father Big A responds, if I did that, he says, it would burn off the top of my head.

June 6

M's Mother on the Telephone

When Eva calls her friend M on the phone, her mother answers.

Can I speak with M? says Eva.

Oh, *caramba*, says M's mother, I am so glad you called. I tried to poo but I could not poo – I even ate broccoli and cauliflower. I tried warm plums with milk, as the doctors recommended.

I'm sorry to hear that, says Eva. Can I speak to M now?

Yes, says M's mother, but I can't talk too loudly because I'm not supposed to talk to her friends about my poo – the problem is that it's been coming out hard as a rock and long, like a curved branch but solid as a brick. It's incredibly painful, and it takes a really long time to finish. So many painful times in the bathroom, you can't imagine. And the hemorrhoids are terrible, unspeakable horror, and not only that but the neighbor – I can hear the neighbor trying to poo from above, and she always turns it into a competition – so now when she wants to brag that she was able to poo, she knocks three times on the floor and I hear the flush. I usually take a broom and knock three times on the ceiling to signal that I poo'ed better than her. But in reality, I tried to poo and tried to poo and tried to poo but I could not make a poo – it was awful.

Can I speak to M now? says Eva.

Oh yes, but my mucus is canary yellow and military green, I must be sick. I mean it's really, really yellow and the doctor said that if my mucus is colorful like this – bright yellow and deep green – I probably have a virus.

June 2015

Today had an idea: keep a journal using my right hand. So far looks nearly almost legible. Good job, non-dominant hand!

Cried today for first time in over a year I think, missing Eva, even though on the way to see her.

A new start at the Newark Int'l airport.

This journaling thing eventually to become a book – one new bad idea for a book each day. No – scrap that. Remember to fix the chronology and tense for flow. Or, at least chronology.

Yoga Un-Catholic

The practice of yoga very well may interfere with our ability to worship, says Archbishop Manuel Johns. In fact, it may conflict with its excessive stretching to reach an un-Catholic state.

June 7

Right Hand Man

Flight delayed overnight. Staying in Newark to avoid trip to and from city. Still feels wrong using non-dominant hand (right). Opened suitcase at hotel, discovered "cedarwood oil" leaked over contact lens eye solution. Disposed of. Remember to call bank tomorrow about Portugal travel. Feeling disabled by writing illegibly without dexterity or precision. Out of control. Spoke with Eva. I love Eva. This look(s) so wrong. Writing 'S' is the hardest letter. Today's crappy novel idea is about a man who learns how to cultivate his sensitive side and (compassionate) by writing a journal with his left hand.

Tomorrow's novel is about a Catholic priest and his tireless efforts to cleanse a Midwestern town of the evils of Yoga. Can't wait to walk the beach in Portugal with Eva.

Remember: revamp resume to reflect description of work duties.

Reminder: do not mention "cedarwood oil" (or Juniper) to Eva – quarrel inevitable.

June 8

Flying to Porto

Woke early – 6:30 am – with another idea for a terrible novel. This one to do with human evolution. Scientists are alarmed by the shrinking y-chromosome – now proven to be respon- sible for the formation of vital organs such as the heart and lungs – but the shrinking has accelerated so that babies all over the world are being born without it – thus normal em- bryonic male development ceases to exist, and within a few years all the natural-born males with vital y-chromosome ge- nomes with it. The solutions for fabricating the human male then must develop impossibly quick – but also the females are dying stillborn because of missing vital chromosomal infor- mation – a kind of inexplicably fast alteration in the genome that scientists attribute to the earth's survival – the earth is cleansing itself of the human race. The earth, in the narra- tive twist, has accelerated adaptation more quickly than the human genome.

Tomorrow's novel consists of one-hundred prefaces to one-hundred absurd, non-existent novels.

June 9

More of the Difficult Hand

Yesterday ended prematurely for me by virtue of my eastbound flight. I am now watching the passenger in front of me give to the stewardess a green pillow stained with either blood or red wine. She attempts to remove the pillowcase, which is on the floor of the carpeted aisle. Digesting the fish (peixe) not the meat (carne) still rumbles. I should be sleeping, like my neighbor, who hates to fly, who has pulled the cadmium red blanket over his face, whose reading light I compassionately switched off. There is that word again, compassion, which brings me to the subject of today's novel idea – the one hundred prefaces. This just may be my worst idea ever – and I am okay with that, but each preface must be voiced with a guiding sense above all things – that while humanity is far from perfect – the base instinct for all is to do good – probably a rip-off of David Hume?

Remember: look into David Hume again.

If I told you I was the kind of guy who wore a suit to a pajama party.

You can sell your time
but you can never buy it back

– Pessoa

June 10

Dia de Camões

I am not yet informed about Dia de Camões. I know only that Camões is the Shakespeare or Shakespear or Shakespere of Portugal, not that the constantly altered the spelling of his name the way Shakspeer or Shekspear did, but that he is canonical. Why we do not have a national holiday for Shakaspare or any other writers? I cannot imagine Wallace Stevens Day closing the doors of Wal-Mart anytime soon. Today's novel is epistolary – an avid reader and octagenarian petitions the U.S. government with touching, personal letters to adopt a national holiday to celebrate Shakespeare – standard modern spelling – despite the fact that Shakespeare was "probably British". In her letters, she explains that she is 87 years old, has ten grandchildren and the complete works of William Shakespeare. Probably the idea was influenced by Eva and Big A's conversation today about grandmothers. He told a story about his friend's grandmother, who in the dark of night would unlock the doors to her daughter's apartment next door, enter the kitchen for a snack without turning on any lights and peek into her granddaughter's room as she was sleeping. This all has nothing to do with Camões, of whom I still know nothing. It has even less to do with Shakespeare except – the grandmother of Big A's friend is descended from British nobility, so yes – no relation to Shakespeare.

But when I was getting dressed I noticed my shirt smelled like "cedarwood oil" (the American version) which in fact is not cedar-derived. The oil comes from juniper, more precisely *juniperus virginianus* – which explains why it resembles gin and for Eva it does not smell like *óleo de cedro* – Portuguese cedar oil, which actually comes from the cedar tree.

About the first scene in the novel idea: a young man, excited to visit his girlfriend for the first time, imagines how she will open the door, dressed in a seductive, semi-transparent silk lingerie – and greet him with a sensual kiss. When he knocks on the door, who answers? Her grandmother, with false teeth, double chin, and an old-fashioned dress like a giant doily. This is the narrator of the epistolary novel called *A Midsummer Night's Grandmother*.

The Newspaper Droolers

It was not an unusual morning, in fact it all started out very typical, mundane, quotidian. When I awoke I had a craving for coffee, as is my habit and my drug – I needed the fix as soon as possible else I would remain in my zombified state of dis-coordination – although that is not a word – un-coordination (also not usually a word), but I would remain non-verbal, nearly without pulse. On this particular morning, I went to the *padaria* close by Eva's – again, nothing out of the ordinary. But I did pick up the newspaper which lives on top of the cigarette machine. I did happen to notice that the paper was fresh from today and not the week-old newspaper that is usually there. So this was envigorating. I dug into the current events. The waitress brought me an espresso without my even asking, and this was unusual. I did not complain. I drank the espresso, and I drank the news. I was almost as thirsty for news as I was for espresso. The espresso was sixty-five cents, but the news was free. A man with a cane – almost a hunchbacked man – bothered me in the middle of my second headline. He wanted to read the paper when I was done. I grunted, or made some similar semi-coherent sound which signals from one man to another that he understands and will comply with said man's request. But there was an anxious tone to the exchange. The crouching man said take your time, but this was understood to be an overly nicety. He did not wish me to take my time. He wished me to hurry up and hand him the newspaper. As I was a visitor in this country and on my best behavior – upstanding member of the neighborhood and all – I got up after scanning over the second article and left the table with newspaper in hand. There he was, the slouching man, famished for journalism, and so I gave him the paper, determined to go elsewhere for more caffeine and more news.

I landed by instinct at the nearest grocery store – the one by the beach on the way to the beachside cafe. I bought my own damn newspaper so that I could lean on it and spill coffee on top of it or drool on it if I wanted to – I could burn a hole through it, or use it as a bib, napkin, whatever. I sat down for another espresso, in the second seat from the window overlooking the road which ran parallel to the sand. I spread out the paper there, and relished for a moment in all the headlines I was about to linger in complete leisure, for hours if I so chose, for this was my paper that I bought with my coins from my pocket and no one else's. It was my property and I had even kept the receipt for some reason. Call that reason instinct.

At this cafe with my newly bought newspaper, the waitress brought me an espresso – she had to ask because I was not that much of a regular, although I could see she recognized me from a few years ago when I had frequented the spot more often than I do now.

Not two seconds after I took the first sip of espresso did an old man with a cane sit in the front seat by the window, but instead of facing the window and the beach just beyond the road – he faced me and my newspaper. He stared at the paper and he watched me read the paper – he even made rustling sounds with his mouth, as if he were imagining what it might be like had he been holding my paper in his hands, and how it might feel. He said something soft and sinister, but it was poorly enunciated and I tried to ignore it as I turned to the sports section. I do not give a rat's ass about the sports section and never did, but I was trying my hardest to ignore the old man. He made more pinching sounds, sucking the life and pleasure out of my reading experience. He coughed, and I heard him say something about newspapers, how there should be more than one newspaper in every cafe. I finished the espresso and could not take the pressure any more. I grasped the receipt for the newspaper, folded it and walked to the counter to pay. He followed. He was pointing at the newspaper.

It's mine, I told him. The newspaper is mine.

But I want to read it, he said.

I bought the newspaper, I explained. Here is the receipt.

But did you finish reading? he said.

The waitress was out in the back garden, and she saw me and the old man at the counter. She came inside, and explained to him that the newspaper was out back, not in my hands. He did not understand. She said she did not know the origin of the newspaper that I held in my hands, but that the cafe's newspaper was out in the garden. I handed two coins to the woman behind the counter, and she returned ten cents too many. In the end, she had paid me to drink the espresso there, but I did not complain. I walked out the back way, just as the old man approached another customer reading the Publico.

I took to the beachside walkway which still was too foggy to actually see the ocean. It was a bleak summer day, grey, and slightly cold, but as I was just waking up from the caffeine I had only noticed the chill. I leaned on the ledge from a vantage point where I could hear the surf beating on the volcanic rock. I opened the sacred paper to the front page one more time. A tap on my shoulder – this time it was a retiree wearing tennis shoes and a jumpsuit.

Driving Job

My driving job is not really a job. The position consists of being on-call twenty-four hours per day and seven days per week, prepared to enact driving duties for Eva (and secondarily but not without frequency, members of Eva's immediate family), conducting both inner city and inter city duties as needed within the Portuguese territories including but not limited to former colonies, island territories and in certain cases or if the need were to arise in the distant or near future, Brazil.

Other duties are understood to be the following:

Driver must be willing to depart within five minutes for any number of destinations with new itineraries to be added without notice. Position includes daily maintenance of a leaking radiator by funneling distilled water into radiator compartment before and after each one way trip of three or more kilometers on sunny days. Driver must abide with itinerary regardless of how indirect or seemingly redundant. On rainy days, radiator fluid must be checked at least once a day. The position is unpaid. Expect evaluations at random to assure quality compliance and best results. Unsatisfactory performance may result in divorce. A good husband can be an appliance-like device, utilized to achieve greater comfort in the household.

June 11, 2015

The Maia Biennale

Four old ladies give directions:

Before the runaround at the exhibition when Eva and I unsuccessfully chased down the four technicians João, Alberto, José, Pedro, and others, to procure cables for a camera, I needed to park the car.

This particular section of Porto is very tight for driving and there is a paucity of spaces to park. So we slowed down and Eva asked for directions. There was a police station that I did not see, where I happened to pause illegally, blocking the police driveway. I was out of earshot, but I could see the four old ladies talking to Eva. One of them had large glasses that were almost goggles, another had a purse bigger than her head. They all seemed extremely exceedingly sweet, but they all four of them were pointing in three different directions and speaking at once. The two in the middle were motioning to the rear of the car, one was gesturing about bumpy terrain or else mountains in the landscape, that might have been on the other side of the moon. All of their mouths were moving at the same time, including Eva's. I could not imagine that any real communication was transpiring, considering the fact that everyone all five women were speaking at the same time. Is this how human communication appears to aliens? But she returned to the car with very clear directions. I do not know how she did it. The first thing she told me, after they had been talking for ten minutes, maybe – was that I have to move the car, or the car will be towed.

June 12

Maybe Tomorrow, Someone

Accompanied Eva to the city hall which was the location for a certain art exhibition to help her set up for her sculptural liquorice and video installation. They scheduled her sculpture to be installed in a semi-intimate closet, but the closet was too small and smelled like a mistreated donkey, so we investigated the premises for more attractive spaces. Most held a condensed and volatile mix of bleach and barnyard.

Finally, we found ourselves on a handicap/wheelchair access ramp that had not seen much use, and Eva with João were discussing camera placement. The camera was to record visitors interacting with her 12-foot liquorice sculpture.

There, said Eva, pointing out a high window ledge. João, ever the sympathetic on-site help, was almost entirely resourceless. He nodded, flipping the battery of the mini-HD camera in and out, in and out. He still had no cables to connect to the monitor. To be fair, we had only been there about six hours. What about the light? I had to ask, as we were conjecturing in the dark. Ah, yes, the light. He flipped the on switch. He shrugged, and it was clear that he could not be expected to know how to change this complicated matter. No light, no video, no cables. We spent the afternoon traversing every corridor, every marble stair in search of the right cables. City hall must be working hard, I thought, to save electricity. At one point, João was cross-examining the inputs on the back of the television using a cigarette lighter.

Maybe tomorrow, he said, someone on the tech team can find a cable that works. He clicked off the lighter. We remained in the darkened basement room, where the videos were to be projected. Projectors were scattered mish-mash across the floor, not connected to anything. The monitor lay mute and dead, the video camera useless without an RCA cable.

Along came Alberto.

Hey Alberto, said João. Have you any cables that would feed live video into this TV?

No idea, said Alberto, but maybe tomorrow someone from tech can do it.

Alberto left.

So, who is on the tech staff? I asked João.

Alberto, he said, and some others, but mostly Alberto.

João escorted us upstairs.

What about this monitor? he said.

João was really sweet. He really did try.

But this takes a different cable, said Eva, looking over the input panel. João ran a finger over the 15-pin RGA female, then peered into the S-Video input. The co-axial threw him into existential despair.

Along came José.

June 13

Another Portuguese Story

Every couple of days, Eva's brother A. will tell me that I should write a story about this or that. A few nights ago, he said: One man, one woman, one world. Think about it, D.

Last night, he reiterated an idea that he has been championing a lot this summer.

A guy has so many cats, he said, he eats the cats. The cats pop up everywhere. He eats more cats. Then, he becomes a cat. Think about it, D.

Then, his brother B. also joined in: A girl who eats sardines, sardines and more sardines. She eats so many sardines that a sardine grows between her legs. Think about it, D.

I thought about it.

June 14

Bolhão

At Bolhão I delivered Eva to the doctor – a specialist in asthma.

I went to a *tasco* nearby to wait. Playing on the television was the Hollywood movie, *48 Hours* – the original. That scene where Eddie Murphy busts up a redneck bar? *That* is my philosophy. I am Eddie Murphy: There's a new sheriff in town, and his name is Reggie Hammond.

Reminder: do not mention "marmalade" to Eva. Guaranteed acridity.

I left the *tasco* – and returned to the doctor's office. The elevator had two doors – the one on the right arrived and I let two ladies enter first. They pressed 4ª *andar* (4th floor) and I pressed 5ª. The elevator was wooden and brass, and smelled like old people. I suppressed a sneeze. It was smaller than a closed shower stall. The elevator began to move, very slowly. Then it stopped. The two ladies were confused.

One asked the other – did you press the 2ª *andar*?

No – I pressed the 4ª. She gasped – she covered her mouth. A bead of sweat slid down the back of her neck. It was completely silent. It was entirely still. None of us moved or said a word or breathed or thought about breathing or thought about moving or thought about saying a word.

Try to stay calm, said her friend. It says "Don't panic" on the wall next to you – look – this elevator always stops on the 2ª *andar*.

Bad idea for a novel: a botanist collects smells and catalogues them in meticulous order with dates and times and descriptions of their odors, planning to mine these for a cookbook. Only his notes are published, posthumously. The notes include a free sample of a new *eau de cologne*.

Near Death Experience with Sardines

Tonight, Eva reminded me of a good story which has me at the butt of the joke – a story we had circulated quite a bit in our first year of marriage because of its high entertainment value.

The story is about how I completely flubbed my first encounter with grilled sardines.

Sardines in Europe, it must be understood, bear almost zero similarity with those the average American might think of when the word is spoken – they are a delicacy eaten fresh, and nobody does it quite like the Portuguese.

Eva took me to a place specializing in grilled fish – close to the fresh fish market just off the port – here one could always see large shipping cargo piling up on the docks and coming in from the sea on freighters of all manner of size. These restaurateurs only answer to locals, though, and I knew this because not long after, I tried going alone and was unable to get a table, unable to even get the waiters to acknowledge me. They brought six perfectly grilled sardines with golden steamed potatoes, red and green peppers plus onions on the side.

I need the bathroom, said Eva, who never ate in restaurants for fear of an allergy attack, and for good reason – I have seen her cheeks swell up like two grapefruits. I began to dissect the closest of the fish. When she returned, I was in the midst of chewing down the whole head and grinding a mouthful of bones – and they were tough bones, too, and required concentration and silence to properly, fully masticate.

Where is the head of the fish? she said. No one eats the head. Why are you eating the bones?

I don't know, but they're really stiff.

Eva remained agape until I gulped a glass of white wine to help the bones flush. By the time I realized my mistake I was half way into the bones, so I had no choice but to continue grinding until I had pulverized and conquered them all. The wine then, saved my life, and Eva taught me to lift the spine straight out with the head and remove it to the side plate so I could access the meat.

But this was not the only time I had acted this way.

Once, we were in Lisbon, at the *tasco* we like to go by the train station and I had ordered the fried cod with onions. Here, she again left off to the bathroom when the food was served. As I had never known fish to be fried with the bones inside, I chomped down on a large chunk and started to munch. But these bones were much stiffer than the sardines I had conquered before. The sound was alarming, and guests could not have missed my foolishness on that day.

Don't tell me you're eating the bones, she said this time as she returned to the table.

Once again, green wine was my savior, as it washed away the bits of what might have easily choked me.

Why didn't you spit it out? she said.

I didn't want to be impolite and spill the food from my mouth.

In my culture, Eva said, you can spit and it's not considered rude.

And that was how I nearly died eating sardines, and once more in Lisbon, chomping down on fried codfish. But I've learned my lesson now – no more bones for me.

June 15

Com-puta-dor

Yesterday, nothing of interest apart from one of my Portuguese language disasters – I have a splitting headache, so I will make it brief.

I wanted to tell Eva's mother that she need not personally wake me – as I downloaded an alarm clock on my "com-puta-dor," but apparently I separated the syllables so that it appeared I was making an eloquent statement that sex with prostitutes causes physical pain.

One more observation – the pseudo-transient man who walks the neighborhood as if carrying a 50 lbs. anvil on his right shoulder – everyone calls him "Tuesday" because whenever asked what day it is, he answers the same – Tuesday. To his defense, I have never seen him beg but he carries that affect, with an oversized t-shirt and beard, and his way of hobbling around the sidewalks as if lost – but then I observe him reach for a key to unlock a gate and disappear inside his house. I can only wonder what his life is really like, or how he gets the flour stains on his clothes.

I am omitting my most intimate thoughts about Eva and Eva's sculptural work because nobody – including my future self – needs to know what private thoughts and feelings I have. My actions should speak to all that – guarding her safety, as it were, Eva asked me to stand outside the offices at her exhibition (city hall) while she used it as a makeshift dressing room. Of all the people I turned away at that door – a musician approached me, arms crossed and balked at the information that she would have to wait a few minutes when I told her, *Eu não falo Português – por favor espera cinco minutos, desculpa* – she asked inhaling and exhaling, what languages do you speak? I answered *Inglês, Francês, Chinês, Espanhol.* She chose Spanish – but was even more flustered when I explained to her that one of the sculptors needed to change her clothes inside and she said had been delayed by "technicians" – I mentioned that Eva had also been delayed by "technicians." It had taken "technicians" three days to arrange a camera in which to record the gallery visitors. Unable to step back, the musician seemed prepared to charge through me when she finally walked away.

June 16

The Mosquitos

The mosquitos went after Eva in her brother's room, and then even at the beach when the wind was so strong she was afraid the umbrellas at the bar "Camelão" would fall over us – again she showed me the red welt the bloodsucker left below her tender shoulder, and another on the tasty meat of her calves. The mosquitos did not care about me – apparently my skin is bitter – but later we were watching Die Hard, the one with Jeremy Irons, and poor Eva shot up from the bed and said, I was just bitten on the foot and mouth. I said, how is that possible? Foot and mouth? How does an insect bite the soles of your feet and then zip up to your face? But she showed me her underlip and there was a bite. Then as she was pulling up her sock to share the damage, she ran to the bathroom calling after her mom. A flurry of Portuguese language does not seem untranslatable anymore – I understood that she was bitten again, this time inside her nostril. She surveyed the mosquito's conquests – ankle, calf, leg, foot, mouth, nostril.

Towards the end of the film, after Bruce Willis shined a searchlight by helicopter on the bad guy's Canadian hideout, the mosquito landed on my kneecap. I observed its flight pattern. The mosquito would touch down, only to lift off right away. Bruce Willis crashed his helicopter and was fumbling with a six-shooter. Then, he was aiming the revolver at Jeremy Irons. The mosquito came again for a rest on my forearm. I knew I only had a millisecond, maybe less to react, so I snapped it with my non-dominant hand.

The mosquito lay still, then it pivoted and began circling with frantic legs and a damaged wing. Bruce Willis fired the shot that snapped the cable that tangled the end of the helicopter and took down Jeremy Irons. The chopper exploded.

Did you get the mosquito? Eva asked.

I flicked my powerful wrist and annhilated the bug. I took it between my fingers to show her I had enacted revenge, my muscles rippling under the light of the television.

Yipee-kai-yay, mother*#&$! said Bruce Willis.

What does yipee-kai-yay mean? Eva said.

It's a cowboy thing, I failed to explain, rinsing my hands in the sink.

The Cleaning Lady and the Potatoes

Just like the day before, and the day before that, C was mopping the floor under the kitchen table – in between pantysqueezing time, a portion of the water let itself down atop a powdery bag of potatoes that lives in the pantry, below the tins of cocoa, the condensed milk, the rice, the sugar packets, the dozens of empty plastic containers wrapped in plastic bags, and the homemade jars of pumpkin and tangerine jam. Only on this third day did Eva's mother notice that the bag of potatoes was wet in parts, and in others had turned fragile and green, a cool algae green with the wrong kind of texture for tubers.

June 15

I was walking the shoreline in the morning – when Eva called to ask if I love her.

Yes, absolutely, I said.

Say it, then.

Say what?

Say that you want to kiss my magnificent golden ass.

I want to kiss your magnificent golden ass.

Say it like there's no tomorrow.

Like there's no tomorrow, I said.

Horrendous idea for a novel called *Express Overnight.* The novel follows a package sent to New York from Porto, a "guaranteed" overnight service.

The package is traceable and follows this path:

Day 1 Porto to Brussels
Day 2 Brussels to Frankfurt
Day 3 Frankfurt to Brussels
Day 4 Brussels to JFK
Day 5 JFK to the Bronx sorting facility
Day 6 Bronx sorting facility back to JFK
Day 7 JFK back to Bronx sorting facility
Day 8 attempted delivery to Hamilton Heights
Day 9 LaGuardia (LGA)
Day 10 Bronx sorting facility
Day 11 lost in transit

June 16

Olive Juice Problem

Remember: ask Eva about the bird clusters which follow the small white fishing boats – I imagine they are chasing the fresh caught fish stored midship or at the back. Remember the sketch I drew on my first trip to Porto, with birds like sparkles of light hovering behind the stern of these boats.

Now – what was the problem of the olive juice. Eva, her brother and I walked to the *Mini Preço* for groceries

– *presunto, chouriço*, olives. I did not know that MSG can be labeled as *intensificação de sabor* on *chouriço*, so I did not bother to notice this was the case with the 1 Euro *chouriço* I picked. It may have been the reason I got sick – but Eva said no, as she pointed out I had eaten hundreds of Chinese meals in New York without comment – but during our evening meal I soaked the black bread (a dense and delicious corn-based bread) in the olive juice, and stupidly ignored her warning not consume the juice from the bag of olives – this was a 1 Euro package of olives I had purchased – saying that the *conservantes* were too strong for the liver. It tasted the same as any olive juice I had eaten in the states without issue, but I had temporarily forgotten that I was not in my own environment, and had no reason to trust my instincts over the reasoning of those around me. I had foolishly failed to heed the edict "When in Rome." I got sick, both with a tremendous headache and stomachache. Eva's mom gave me a white pill as I writhed in her brother's room. After a nap, my headache cleared up and I could descend to the kitchen, as her mom was preparing a chicken soup. Her father opened the fridge and showed me the ingredients on the pack of olives: E-270, E-273, E-275.

These chemicals are incredibly strong, he said.

As he was explaining, he hovered a peach above a glass of water. With ordinary water, he said, this fruit would become rotten. But with E-270, with just one drop of E-270 in this glass, the peach could be preserved for six years. That is how strong E-270 is, he said. I understood what he was saying, but somehow in the mélange of English-Spanish-Portuguese-French through which we communicate, "*another-chose*" is one of his common phrases – a mishmash of French and English from the phrase "*quelque chose*."

It slipped my memory the correct word for preservatives in Spanish and Portuguese is a false cognate – and one of the worst to forget – so when I said I understood, that I had eaten *"demasiados preservativos,"* I recognized too late that I told my stepfather I had become sick from eating too many condoms.

June 17

Remembering How Communication Works

-------------------------------CÓDIGO----------------------------

codificação>>>>>>>>>   <<<<<<<<<<descodificação

^(MENSAGEM)^

EMISSOR-------->>--------->>--------->>---------->>RECEPTOR

canal de comunicação

June 18

Beard in the Cake

Remember: go to a favorita do Boa Vista for gifts.

There are events which upset Eva that make no sense to me whatsoever but must seem utterly comical when noted on paper – take for example today, we were about to go look at frames for new glasses, because my glasses broke apart and I had no backup pair. When I told her I would shave and we could go in 5 minutes (we were also waiting for mom to finish a long phone call) she suddenly started yelling that I would get the beard hairs in the cake batter if I shaved, and that she would now refuse to go with me to find eyeglasses. I complained that it is impossible for my hairs to jump from the drain in the bathroom sink, walk into the hallway into the kitchen to insert themselves into a bowl of cake mix on the counter, but she insisted that if I were to shave now, the cake would be filled with hairs from my beard, and this also cancelled out my ability to purchase prescription eyewear.

Last night, Eva was impressed by my crepe-making abilities. Today, she is certain that shaving absolves me from putting my chin anywhere near a cake. I must be missing some vital information or else the signifier and signified were not decoded properly from either her part or mine – perhaps both. Did she think I wanted to shave with the cake batter?

June 20

The 1ˢᵗ Anniversary of Our Wedding and Disastrous Lunch Party

Yesterday was a full day of potential stories.

This always happens to me and then I feel destroyed and demoralized from spending the last five hours crushed against the wall of Eva's bed.

"D. Zombie" is what her father called me because I was so tired I was unable to speak. This is untenable. Eva's older brother B. was visiting from Madrid, and has taken the room I was sleeping in.

Therefore, I spent last night squeezed into a space so small I was not aware the body could become quite that small.

The representation of space, with some, but not much hyperbole, claimed in the bed looked like this:

EEEEEEEEEEEEEEEEEEEEEEEEEEEEEEEEE
EEEEEEEEEEEEEEEEEEEEEEEEEEEEEEEEE
EEEEEEEEEEEEEEEEEEEEEEEEEEEEEEEEE
EEEEEEEEEEEEEEEEEEEEEEEEEEEEEEEEE
EEEEEEEEEEEEEEEEEEEEEEEEEEEEEEEEE
EEEEEEEEEEEEEEEEEEEEEEEEEEEEEEEEE
EEEEEEEEEEEEEEEEEEEEEEEEEEEEEEEEE
EEEEEEEEEEEEEEEEEEEEEEEEEEEEEEEEE
EEEEEEEEEEEEEEEEEEEEEEEEEEEEEEEEE
EEEEEEEEEEEEEEEEEEEEEEEEEEEEEEEEE
EEEEEEEEEEEEEEEEEEEEEEEEEEEEEEEEE
EEEEEEEEEEEEEEEEEEEEEEEEEEEEEEEEE
EEEEEEEEEEEEEEEEEEEEEEEEEEEEEEEEE
EEEEEEEEEEEEEEEEEEEEEEEEEEEEEEEEE
EEEEEEEEEEEEEEEEEEEEEEEEEEEEEEEEE
EEEEEEEEEEEEEEEEEEEEEEEEEEEEEEE
EEEEEEEEEEEEEEEEEEEEEEEEEEEEEEEEE
EEEEEEEEEEEEEEEEEEEEEEEEEEEEEEEEE
EEEEEEEEEEEEEEEEEEEEEEEEEEEEEEEEE
EEEEEEEEEEEEE EEEEEEEEEEEE
EEEEEEE me EEEEEEEEE
(wall) (wall) (wall) (wall) (wall) (wall) (wall)

The irony is that the entire night, Eva complains I am keeping her awake, but I cannot move and my body feels annihilated. It is difficult to express the extent to which I cannot function now as a result of that immobility – it is like the most oppressive hangover but without the drink – the problem is that the family is coming for lunch to celebrate our one year anniversary of marriage and I do not think I will be in anything resembling a sociable mood. Not only does my lower back hurt, my shoulders hurt. My neck hurts. My ears hurt from being shoved into the wall. The best part is how she makes it like I am preventing her from a good night's rest. It will take hours of stretching to undo the damage.

Later that same night, cutey Eva gets bitten by mosquito five more times on her neck. My grandmother used to say that mosquitos only like the sweetest skin, and I think she was true.

I hesitate to mention this because it does not reflect well on me, and is completely my fault – but at the lunch party I missed my opportunity to make a toast. The disorientation caused by all my things which seem to be misplaced by the cleaning lady or perhaps others – the poem I prepared for the toast was tucked into a notebook in my leather jacket, which disappeared minutes before people began to arrive for the luncheon. My suit was misplaced somewhere, so unreachable it may as well have been draped over the edge of a tourist boat on the Douro river.

Being the dutiful husband, it was my role to greet family as they came in, although I could barely stand, being so tired from the bedroom ordeal. It gives fresh meaning to the phrase *I have a crush on you.*

The Sock Missile

Today I hit my head on a cutting board which was inexplicably located on a shelf crowded with detergents, sponges, and other shampoos and cleaning miscellanea on the window in the lower bathroom. I was splashing my face with water when I reared up to find a towel, and plunked my head onto a corner of the hardened plastic. The bump on my head is very unpleasant.

Eva has a habit of throwing worn clothes from the second floor, where the bedrooms are located, down onto the stairs.

The stairs are the repository for discarded objects which are about to be forever misplaced by the cleaning lady. Everyone in the house knows that a pair of new shoes placed strategically on the second to last stair will eventually be relocated to the closet of disappearances. This imaginary closet is located only in the minds and memories of each member of the family, wherein their long-lost perfume, hand cream, computer mouse or bracelet has gone to make its final stand in a department store for the forgotten. I have mourned over a pair of jeans, shiny black shoes, a silver fountain pen. This closet is not to be confused with the closely-related cabinet under the stairs, from where objects are temporarily jumbled together with a mere fifty percent chance of being hurled into a quasar.

But today when Eva threw her used socks into the well, I was untying the shoelaces on my Italian running shoes (a no-name, replaceable pair of shoes) when I looked skywards out of some long learned instinct – call it love – to discover that my mouth was the perfect landing pad for a pair of Eva's hot pink smurfette motif (89% cotton 5% polyester 7% lycra) crew socks.

The cutting board injury faded at that point, replaced squarely with the image of her feet coverings on my lips.

June 22

A Hotel in Foz (post-anniversaire)

The smallest creature at this hotel breakfast buffet issues the blaringest, the most shrill and nail-splitting frequencies repeatedly, relentlessly, ferociously – are the parents as oblivious as they appear? I gathered they're from Spain, but are they so absorbed with their smartphones to notice or care how everyone might be affected by this defenseless, hairless, fathomless, not yet even remotely linguistic clod of nerves, ligaments, cartilage and half-formed DNA sequences – an animal so tiny it doubles in size every ten minutes. This savage mammal has lungs the size of my hands – no – smaller, and yet its vocal capacity is so overwhelming that it could drown a jackhammer, halt production of an automobile factory, trigger alarms at any bank, instill anxiety in any postal worker. Such is the fear-factor of this tiniest of humanoids – surely alien life forms observing these parents' behavior would think that human beings shrink down to the size of a peach as they mature – it would be one possible explanation why they treat with such reverence this rude, obnoxious biped not one quarter their stature – this creature who not only talks over everyone but defames those guests wholly unconnected, yes – assaults pure strangers with his monosyllabic performance all the while sprouting lactose from his nostril and vomiting apple puree as his devotees pamper every orifice with perfumed towels. I have to hand it to these parents – they sure know how to spoil a child.

Now returning to the hotel room after breakfast, Eva has removed her clothes, and is gone. No note, just the lingering sense of the last argument, and gone.

This is why:

Last night, Eva informed me that I had failed as a host for the anniversary luncheon. It is my understanding that my role was to meet and greet — but when I was so tired from being crushed in the bedroom, it was impossible to remain standing and conversant the entire time. I also did not see her play this role, as she was seated talking to B on the couch while I fumbled socially to try and entertain. I know that I failed, but the pettiness inside me continues to complain that I learned only after the party how I was expected to open the door for everyone — the pettiness nags that it is only possible to influence a person's behavior before an event. Eva's approach was to communicate her disappointment afterwards. I think it is a miracle we are together as a couple — one smile from her and I forget fifty slanders, like the biggest fool between earth and mars.

But here is a story: after the party there was a lot of commotion about where I would sleep, and the flowers causing Eva breathing problems. In my mind, her parents seemed upset that Eva wanted the flowers thrown out. They seemed to be arguing passionately over this, but in reality, my understanding of Portuguese is twisted and frequently offbase — I might ask Eva later and she could say they were discussing the price of octopus. I can no longer trust my ears or my eyes when it comes to occurrences in this land.

Eva summarized for me that either the flowers stay in the living area or I will sleep there, but not both. Out of politeness I did not interject but I did not see the logic behind either keeping the flowers in light of Eva's asthma, or moving them to the kitchen, which is what they did, or moving them to the foyer, where Eva would almost certainly be affected. I watched as they argued, bouncing the bright golden flowers from room to room, the tightly bound white buds with green ribbons dripping with pollen, into the kitchen, the foyer, again to the livingroom, the bathroom, and finally back to the kitchen, as Eva retreated upstairs to higher ground. Another aspect I did not understand was that either the flowers go into the foyer or the kitchen or I cannot sleep in the livingroom. Her mother had set up the cot there because everyone knew how Eva's sleeping patterns are impossible to tolerate — Big A told me it was the same when she was a child — she would not allow him an inch on the bed. She dominated the bed so that he could not move at all — and had to be utterly silent even with regards to breathing. This was the reason I had not slept at all the previous night, because not only was I stiff from not moving and sticking to the wall, I was holding my breath the entire night. Every time I breathed too loudly, she would shake me, and say, You breathe too loud. Stop breathing.

My story and Big A's story matched up. We traded knowing looks in the morning, when I emerged with a crooked neck and earned the nickname "Zombie-D." But the case of the flowers I did not understand. Were they afraid I would kill the flowers if I slept next to them, the way her cousin P. had once caused an entire vase of magnolias to wilt overnight, as the story goes, because of the famous reeking odor from his stained-with-sweat-never-changed sneakers? Apparently so. Thus, I joined Eva upstairs so we might look for a hotel online — one we had been to the previous year, just after the wedding, as a kind of mini-honeymoon. This upset Eva's brother B, who travelled from Madrid to be with family. Now it seemed like everyone was upset. I booked the hotel beginning the following day, in hopes that brother B might calm down. They went for a midnight walk and I went to the livingroom cot — the flowers remained on the window sill in the kitchen.

How did I end up alone in the hotel on this day after the day after the first anniversary? I can only recount what happened up to this point with the caveat that Eva is fond of dramatic exits. She has two specialties cultivated in the course of our marriage — one is getting severely upset and the other is storming out of the hotel, house, apartment, you name it — which might be exasperating for others, but for me gives way to the adorable. The frequency with which she does this is such that it has a normalizing effect. Eighty percent of the time, she is upset if awakened before two in the afternoon because she must always sleep until 2 pm, or nearly so.

We had agreed the night before over chorizo and champagne that I should call the front desk for a 9 am wake up call. But this never happened.

Let me back up to the check-in, in which Eva thinks there was a misunderstanding between us and the concierge, a feminine kind of man, who (according to Eva's interpretation of events) was probably under the impression that she was a high-class prostitute, and I was her customer. The reason, Eva explained, was that there were two types of prostitutes in Portugal – a local type, usually overweight with no teeth – and a less unattractive, more expensive prostitute who goes with businessmen at business hotels like the one we checked into. She had then made what she called a normal amount of small talk with the concierge. He had been to New York recently and was set to go again – she had always preferred the food in Portugal because artificial coloring and additives agitates her fragile digestive system. Later, while we were in the swimming pool, the concierge had given her a kind of look that involved excessive eyebrow movement that she found curious. For these reasons, the fact I was a US citizen from New York who showed him a NY license instead of a passport, coupled with her local accent – and for this, Eva concluded that he thought of her as an upper crust hire. That, and the fact that he had said we would have to pay for the entire night, even as he hinted that we might only need the room for a couple of hours.

Now, imagine this concierge and another staff member notices me going to the breakfast room alone the following morning. Then, I stayed in the lobby waiting until at least 12 noon because I thought that she had gone back to sleep and

Eva must have snuck past me while I was in the lounge, or else walked right out the revolving doors while I was getting my cilias burned by the megaphone baby from Madrid. But if the concierge suspected that we had a transactional relationship, that suspicion was solidified when she left without me, as I remained bleary-eyed with coldcuts, jams and croissants, being tortured by the Prince of the Prado.

Will she return? I have no idea, and meanwhile I am checked in for two nights. She had swigged the remaining half bottle of champagne, grabbed her backpack and left. Completing this scenario, Eva tells me later that her brother A — who was en route to a funeral in dark sunglasses and suit, and who had dropped us off in a black car with tinted windows — might have looked like the pimp.

June 22

Idea for a new novel today.
It starts like this:
I have a deep and terrible secret.
I cannot write without stealing words from the mouths of those I love.

June 23 or 24?

The fact I do not know what day it is exists as a testament to how fortunate I am — but it is the kind of fortunate which is not secure in the sense of material riches as the word fortune might imply, but rather a happiness dependant upon gratitude for the time I do have. Here is the sea — here is a man who gazes upon the windsurfers and the beach strollers with a full stomach, a notebook and pen. Correction: two pens. Last night, a poet asked if he could borrow a pen from me. I told him I always carry one – no, two. Then I remarked that although I had met him years ago I had never read his work. Neither have I, he said – and that's when I realized he must be a very talented poet. This was at S. João, Porto's biggest celebration of the summer, maybe of the whole year. He wrote a few words on his name card, then gave it to an Afro-Brazilian pianist from São Paulo. There were many like-minded folks of this ilk at the party, and for the purposes of conversation this was easy and alternately hard. Two composers might be exchanging details about their art collection like so many ping-pong balls, for example, hypothetically:

I have an Angelo, and four Lygia Papes.

I also have a few Lygia Papes, and two Angelos.

June 24 or 25

This afternoon, my dear cuteness Eva spent the lunch hour complaining to her family, then to me that the secretary at the University had delayed her paperwork again for a scholarship. I offered to let her use my computer to call New York, and I was met with vicious yelling, vitriol. I thought, isn't it strange that I have arrived to find this conversation normal? The lantern/balloon I bought for flight at St. Joao was so big, when it lifted off the ground it tilted against a light pole, nearly caught fire then climbed over the houses nearby only to descend in a flaming ball of wax before it left the neighborhood. I have heard it is a symbol of bad luck.

As David Hume once wrote, Liberty is the ability to construct walls of one's own particular prison and recognize the intricacy of its design with a detachment so profound it might have been built by someone else.

Seven new GMO crops have been approved for EU import. I am terrified that this will be the end of decent food here in Europe, which has been seemingly the last stand against GMO foods. Within ten years, I predict that food will be tasteless everywhere. GMO crops in Spain will cross the borders into Portugal, chickens fed on the new GMO crops will develop only through hormone treatments, etc. Goodbye good food.

June 24

The Fisherwoman and the Seagull

Eva's mother takes me to visit the fisherwoman.

The fisherwoman illegally sells freshly caught fish from a white van parked on a sidestreet a few blocks back from the red and white striped lighthouse.

On top of the van is a white seagull with a dirty grey patch on its backside, pacing back and forth on the roof.

Her husband keeps watch on the activity of the street halfway up the block. He greets Eva's mother as we approach – I think she has *linguado* today. No octopus this time.

Oh, good, says Eva's mother, I was hoping for *linguado*.

Because I know how much you like the octopus, says the husband.

As we approach, the seagull squawks, continues pacing on top of the van. A customer finishes paying, and the fisherwoman hands the customer a coin.

She's hungry, says Eva's mother, referring to the bird.

Yes, says the fisherwoman, she's always stalking me.

Today we have *linguado* fresh caught, says the fisherwoman, showing Eva's mother a cut of the fish. The fish is long, earthy, and flat. Eva's mother walks away with a plastic bag, all fish caught fresh this morning.

The fisherwoman yanks on a different cut of fish, *pescado*, and drops the scales and other scraps on the back bumper of the van. The seagull crawls over the back window and sticks its beak into the pile of guts.

After we return to the house, Eva and I pause at the closest neighborhood cafe to get an ice cream. We decide to stroll along the beach while the crowds are thinner at lunchtime. As we cross the street and I unwrap the chocolate bar, a long streak of wetness splatters atop the ice-cream from overhead. Part of it gets the back of my hand. A seagull complains from up above, and I deposit the tainted dessert in a green container on the corner.

That's good luck, says Eva, not missing a single step.

Just Peachy

I am munching on Spanish ribs, drinking a glass of peach juice. It is not 100% juice, but there is a high content of juice in my glass. I am alone in the kitchen, a feat so rare the experience takes on an eerie quality, as if I were inhabiting a parallel universe where being alone might be possible.

Then, the spell is broken. Eva's brother A walks into the kitchen, deposits a plastic bottle in the recycling. He peels a banana and eats it with a rapidity I have never seen, then puts the banana in the trash. I continue to eat in silence. A calls out to his mother as he leaves the kitchen.

Mom, he says, D is drinking juice in the kitchen. You know I can't take the smell of juice so I can't stay in the kitchen.

I quickly rinse out my glass of juice.

After a few minutes, Eva comes down to join me, sitting on her designated chair at the head of the table. She nudges the table forward an inch, and my plate along with it. I adjust my chair accordingly.

My brother, she says, wanted to keep you company while you eat but he gets anxiety from the smell of fruit juice. So he complained to his mom, because he did not know what to do.

I know – I heard what he said. But why didn't he say it to me? I would just rinse the glass and never drink juice again.

I'm not sure, but my guess is that he doesn't feel comfortable.

June 26

Boo is Bad

Argument last night so painful and humiliating I am considering not only leaving Portugal but our lives together – all because I wanted to call her "bubu" – what for me is a term of endearment. Her response was to call me "piece of – ," an insult so horrible I am still jammed-up with seething the following morning. So many difficulties in living with Eva that I continually think about leaving – "no water noise" in the morning means I am unable to wake up and splash water on my face or even brush my teeth or make coffee without receiving an endless stream of hateful invectives. I am filled with pettiness. But it is the kind of insult that is hard to shake, and now I have absolutely no sympathy in my head. I am at "Cafe

Impathio," a misspelling which overlooks the Atlantic. The sea is calm, bluer than yesterday. Two clippers line the horizon. It is mid-morning, and the crowds are beginning to curdle the esplanade, kids and their toys, dogs, old men with bellies and cars tagged with Picasso's signature.

Eva wakes from a nap and pokes me, terrified with nightmares: you were holding a chicken, she says, under your arms. It was a service animal.

And I could only eat the square-shaped eggs from your chicken. And the doctor kept trying to get me to eat the egg-shaped eggs, which I am allergic to. What an absolute nightmare.

June 28

Sunday with Grandma

This Sunday, just like every Sunday, grandma comes to have lunch with us at the house, then we take a nap in the living room (her legs supported upon the footstools in the middle, mine across the floor), then by the time the sun is setting we play a paired card game called *Sueca* (translation: Swedish Woman) in which I do not participate but only observe as just about everyone raises their voices so that grandma can hear which is the 'trump' card at least once per game, then we take her home around midnight. Grandma invariably plays at least one card out of turn, and counts the cards off under the table like a gangster. She wears sunglasses throughout the game, giving the impression that she is both deaf and blind.

When the time comes to leave, I get the driver's seat, with Eva's mother navigating the thruway from Foz to central Porto.

Outside grandma's building, garbage is strewn along the sidewalk, spilled over from a nearby dumpster. The hallway entrance is dark, and the light does not seem to be functioning. We cram into the shoe-sized elevator, close the iron gate, press the 3rd floor button. The elevator shakes violently, then begins to move.

And this time, like almost every time, grandma shows me around the house as if I had never been there.

And this, she says, opening the cabinet below the Holland beer steins, this is our Staffordshire service. It is a complete service, she says, all the plates for a three course meal with dessert, with all the silverware intact.

I remember.

And this, she says, is furniture which one can only find in museums. And look at this grandfather clock, she says. This mirror: look at the detail of that woodwork.

I remember. I have been visiting for more than a year since our marriage.

Mom, he's already seen the house any number of times, Eva's mother says from down the long hallway. You gave him the tour last year.

Look at these chairs, says grandma, they don't make them with this pattern handmade in leather anymore. One cannot find this but in museums, she says.

Yes, I say. I remember the wonderful handiwork.

Only in museums, says grandma. Here, she says, is a slightly different design of a chair. Look at these carvings. Have you ever seen an ivory tusk like this made from a gigantic elephant? This is illegal so they don't make these anymore.

I remember. This is still incredible stuff. The details are impressive.

Mom, says Eva's mother from the back bedroom, he's already been here several times.

Teapots from Russia, Japan, original design, grandma says. She opens a glass cabinet and turns over a candy dish. What year does this say?

1854 or 1654, it's hard to tell.

Look at this antique map of Porto, she says, pointing to the wall across from the kitchen. Original, hundreds of years old. This is drawn by hand, signed by the artist.

I love the details of this piece.

Have you seen a map like this anywhere else? she says. It's not made with a machine, but with a human hand.

It's really gorgeous.

You can only find this in museums, she says. Look at the signature.

I couldn't agree more.

Over here is the kitchen, grandma says, continuing the tour. Everything clean, organized, sparkling. Look here, she says. It's spotless, like a museum.

Eva's mom is cutting her medications in half portions, leaving them in pill boxes on the kitchen table. On the way down the stairs in total darkness, I have to grip the railing because I cannot see anything.

June 29

Pass the Pimple

Unfortunately, I must really be in love because I did not leave her and probably forgave her for the "piece of – " escapade. The hellish outweighs the heavenly but if she gives me heaven for one hour somehow I tolerate hell for weeks and weeks.

Like the way she invents games – "Pass the Pimple" is her latest. She has a breakout rash of something resembling measles, which I may contract – and she rubs her belly against mine – or rubs her feet along my legs and laughs without sound. To see her so deeply entertained – occasionally a tiny peep escapes – is to experience the highest delight. Also she enjoyed my mispronunciation of Portuguese again. This time it was the word for "straw" which I mispronounced and no matter how many times her cousin P. trained my ear to hear the word correctly, I always managed to say "dick" instead of "straw". It only has a slightly different "l" sound, or so it seemed to me. Then, I showed Eva my grammar book. I bought it in a grocery store. It is called *Ratinho*, but she said the way I pronounced it was slang for the female human reproductive organ.

June 29

Today in my notebook I found a note from Eva. I do not remember when or why it addressed this issue:

If you love me kiss my ass with your hands dry

June 30

No Oranges

Today we are eating Spanish squid with olive oil and boiled potatoes. It is a meal which I cannot say that I enjoy – its legs have a thin layer of translucent slime, they are violet colored with tiny suckers, and it has a flavor resembling dirt, light detergent, and fermented soy with an aftertaste of cheap vodka. The oven is making its usual hiccupping sound like a drowning duck.

Eva uses a prodigious amount of olive oil on top of her potatoes. Her brother A uses no salt, no olive oil, nothing. Her mother waits for us to finish eating before ripping up fresh parsley and whipping it over a plate of spaghetti.

We sit in relative silence, then A reaches for a banana.

Mom, he says, these bananas are way too green. Why do you always buy bananas so green? And why do you buy so many bananas? Nobody will ever eat this many bananas. There must be twenty-five bananas here.

When they ripen, she says, you can eat them.

I reach over the fruit basket for an orange. As I begin to peel the orange, Eva pushes back her chair hard, which screeches along the tile. The sound of the oven comes to a halt.

The smell makes me vomit, Eva says.

What smell?

The orange smell. When you finish let me know and I will keep you company again.

What? I didn't know you had issues with oranges.

Well, says Eva, now you know. While you're at it, take out the garbage with the orange peels when you're finished.

Okay.

June 30

The Grocery Stalker

Eva's mother asked us to stop by the grocery, as we were about to drive beachside anyway and would be passing the store. I carried a pink plastic bag and Eva took a triangular ticket at the butcher's counter, #755. There were three workers behind the chopping blocks: one was mopping the floor, one was tidying up the back cooler, and the last was running a rag over the countertop, but slowly, like she was allergic to sudden movement. There was a line of six people waiting. The LED readout was stuck on "serving customer #50." Nobody was being served.

A girl wearing all black walked in front of Eva at very close range, crossing the window of raw pork *entremeada*. Eva then moved to the cheese display, and the girl appeared again, scooting her hips just to Eva's front, practically rubbing her back end on Eva's skirt. Eva moved to the *Alheira* and *Farinheira* chorizo display. There was still nobody being served at the butcher's counter.

I went to the checkout, with my yogurt and carbonated water. I noticed Eva by the ice cream bars closely checking labels. The girl again was there, this time at Eva's back, and reached for a box just below Eva's navel area. The girl looked over the box, then returned it to the same location, passing her hand over the frills in the front of Eva's skirt. Eva closed the door and added the ice cream to my groceries at checkout. The girl followed us out the door, looked at Eva as if to say something, and then didn't.

The last thing I saw before we left was the line at the butcher counter had doubled, but the sign still read "serving customer #50."

Preface #87

The Elder Gropings: An Ethnography of Fifty Testimonies

I hope this introduction should suffice to establish the most genuine and fullest background setting for how groping is perpetrated by elder females in Portugal – to relate just how relatively common these occurrences are – I estimate – and this is backed numerous studies herein enclosed – that groping by these older ladies who choose young men as their victims is more frequent in Portugal than in the United States by more than one-hundred thousand fold (see Appendix B).

That said, the fifty testimonies in this book were complied from oral histories of males as young as twelve and as old as eighty-seven years of age. The ages of these subjects as they were interviewed for this book do not reflect the age in which they experienced the groping – that is, an 87-year old man may have related stories from when he was 16 and was groped the first time he entered a movie theater.

It should be stated also, in this introduction, that by "Elder Gropings" the authors herein refer not to Elders in the Mormon Church (or the Church of Latter Day Saints/LDS) and by the use of the word Elders do not mean to signify or reference whatsoever to said church or agents of said church. Here, the term "elder" signifies only those persons for whom it may be said they have reached a senior age, generally known to denote persons over the age of 65.

Some commonalities among the gropings: these partic-ular stories always involve a much older female groper (50 years or more greater in age than the victims), and a younger male victim. This is not to say that other age/sex combinations do not occur in Portugal or elsewhere, only that they are not the focus of this study.

Gropings and the role of place: the authors have noted an increasing frequency of groping at events of "high culture" such as museums, galleries, and theatres.

Social status of gropers, victims: the range of class seems to be dependent on the location of the groping, such that higher class gropers seem to congregate where there are cultural events, whereas the lower classes of gropers seem to be channeling their activities in more common, accessible areas. Definitions of "higher" and "lower" class are determined solely by interviews with the victims. For the purposes of this study, subjects were told to draw their own conclusions as to the meaning of the phrases "higher class" and "lower class."

The authors of this book do not claim to make judgments on the psychology or "perversion" of these acts, either as pertains to the significantly older female gropers nor the significantly younger male victims, regardless of their various testimonies in which there was found to be a surprising number from both parties who derived some form of positive result or pleasure from said acts. Nor is it the role of the authors herein to make any overstatements with regards to the meaning of the words "pleasure," "positive result" or "perversion." These descriptive words are taken from the testimonies themselves and archived in the data tables as represented in Appendix C. These above potentialities are among those *not to be argued.*

July 5

An Even Worse Conversation I Hoped to Avoid

It was during lunchtime, and Eva's mother had prepared a lemon chicken in the oven. I was scooping the rice into my plate when Eva volunteered a class of information that I had again, erroneously assumed was private. I had earlier confided in her that my bowel movements were occurring at the rate of twice per diem, and that they were smooth and trouble-free. I was already turning red even my elbows were blushing.

Eva then asked her father – who was also available to partake in this lively public discussion of best practices for my eliminatory procedures – if it were excessive to be regular twice a day.

Well, said Big A, has he been eating tomatoes? Because tomatoes like these will do that, he said, pointing to the eight or ten downturned tomatoes, called Bull's Heart tomatoes, which were ripening in a milk crate on the floor next to the fridge.

Yes, said Eva, he eats them a couple times each day.

Well, said Eva's mother, then obviously he is pooping with frequency because of the tomatoes. It's not diarrhea is it?

No, said Eva. He doesn't have diarrhea.

Did he poop that much in the states? Asked Big A.

Eva turned to me and asked. I could feel my tongue going completely dry in my mouth from shame. I could barely speak.

Slowly, with my tongue sticking to the sides of my mouth, I said, normally I go about once a day or every two days.

Yes, said Eva's brother A, your husband is visiting the bathroom because of the tomatoes. Is the poop unusually smooth? he asked.

That's what I wanted to ask, said Big A. Tell us about the consistency of the poo.

Yes, said Eva, that's exactly what he said. It's really smooth and delivers with ease.

Grandmother entered the room, balancing her 98 years on the back of the folding chair in the crowded kitchen. What's that? she said.

We were talking about why D is crapping twice a day while in Portugal, said A. And the poo is effortless.

What? Speak up, said grandma.

We are talking about D's feces, said A, with a much louder voice.

What? said grandma.

Eva's mother intervened, speaking more loudly than I had ever heard anyone speak in the house. At this point I start to feel faint in the head.

Mom, she said, raising her voice so loud that any passerby, even across the street, would hear through the kitchen windows. Eva's husband goes to the crapper two times each day.

Grandma's interest is peaked, and said, that sounds normal to me. Is he eating tomatoes? Because that can make things much finer.

Yes, says Big A, he eats these tomatoes which is why we think he is doing it twice a day.

What? said grandma, once more lost.

Eva's mother set down a kitchen rag and approached grandma's ears. We think it's the tomatoes, she screamed. That's what's making him poop so much.

Oh, definitely, said grandma. It's not diarrhea, is it?

No, mom. It's not diarrhea.

What?

It's coming out solid, Eva's mother said, once again amplifying next to grandma's ear. It's coming out in smooth but solid chunks.

What?

D's poo is smooth but solid, mom. Smooth but solid.

Ah, grandma said, finally getting the whole picture. It's good to be young, she said.

I have no idea what kind of expression I was wearing on my face, but grandma looked at me and winked.

On the subject of my bowels, the entire family was in perfect accord.

July 9

A few days in Lisbon without my journal was great and terrible – Lisbon was tremendous, but not having a place to take notes was awful. Eva's gigantic liquorice underwear sculptures on exhibition at the MAAT. My Portuguese is improving. Yesterday, when we arrived at the Porto train station and found her brother's car, I attempted to say *vamos emborrrrra* but rolling the "r's" too much. Instead of "let's go" apparently I said "let's poop" because of my beautiful accent.

July 9

Baratas Baratas / Cheap Cockroaches

Two nights ago was Eva's gallery opening, a huge success. A steady stream of people came into the MAAT to see her sculptures – and during my reading – a collage of Pessoa's heteronyms and a short story about an American in Lisbon who sits by the bronze statue of Pessoa every day to complain, lovingly, about his wife.

But after the opening is when the good stuff began. Piled into N's car, we attempted parking in Rossio, but the hills too steep, narrow and packed spit us into a parking garage.

The *tasquinha* where N took us was a real gem – the owner tended over us with rhyming couplets, a Portuguese tradition now dying with the handful of grandfathers who maintain this oral treasure:

What would you like to drink?

Beer is no good for your health, I think.

Wine is slightly better but no matter,

with either one you'll get much fatter!

I only tell you because you're my friend.

and do not want you to meet an early end.

The owner danced around our table and with each request, the owner rebutted in perfect rhyme, with a high-pitched song and moving quick, hands changing tablecloths and placing forks and knives for the five of us – B., N, J, Eva and myself.

Bife a Casa was their order and Eva suggested I follow – a grilled steak with a fried egg on top and French fries. N told me of the 1755 earthquake, where the people of Lisbon ran into the open square (*Pombal?*) below the *tasquinha* for safety – little did they know a tsunami wave would rise above the square to swallow them. I could feel the sadness of loss was visceral for him by the way he described it, and I saw how N could carry this oral tradition of rhyming – he is a tremendous storyteller.

With N, I felt as if I knew him all my life – probably because he and J are so close with Eva and have been for so long – only he was drinking and I was not. For dessert, a secret nun's recipe – egg yoke pudding which N said was purported to contain the sweat of virgins. But this would stand to logic, I said, if it were made by nuns. Then as I was halfway through, the *barata* (a baby roach, likely) appeared from somewhere in the middle of the table – and scurried unafraid underneath N's plate and around his snifter of *aguardente*. I was the only one to spot the creature since I was sober as a cat. When it came out crawling towards Eva, N slapped it with his hand to kill it, and said, mmmmm, good protein.

July 10

The Hospital and the Fisherman

Back in Porto, I was requested to drive again – this time Eva wanted me to drive her to the hospital to check her rash. She had been getting red spots for two weeks, and was unsuccessful in transferring the disease over to me with her pass-the-pimple attempt. Eva is a person whose state of health is so fragile that if I were a stranger, I would take her to be a hypochondriac. She is not. The fact is that she is today also suffering from diarrhea, which unfortunately, is a common state of being for Eva.

However, I believe that her health influences her state of mind, and when giving driving directions we always manage a multiplicity of creative ways to miss the correct route. This time, she invariably confounded me by pointing to the right and saying *left!* in a highly emotional, blistering tone. On a different street, while I was in the process of turning left into an intersection in which there was an immediate left/right turn decision required, and she yelled, *straight ahead forever!* Arguments ensued, spurning other arguments within the larger fight. One of these reccurring arguments is about the meaning of *straight ahead forever* on a curved road. I claimed it's better for her to give directions in Portuguese because she does not remember the English word *stoplight*, for instance, so instead of stoplight she frantically said *the blinking, the blinking*, which seemed to border on the nonsensical. This is not to mention that she confused left and right both before and after the intersection. Twice, after we had already passed an intersection she said – you missed the turn! She had just forgotten to mention anything about a turn until it was too late. It is time for me to upgrade my language skills.

Eventually, miraculously, we parked in the hospital parking lot, across from the metro tracks, with her mother asking us to be *calma, calma,* because after being screamed at with faulty directions, I snapped and must have raised my voice. Walking up the hill to the hospital I saw a child with no arms – his left stub just a bit rounder and four or five inches longer than his right. This shut me up, and I returned, again, to a proper state of gratitude.

One thing I almost forgot – Big A told me a story last night in the kitchen. We had just finished eating a *pescada* fried with eggs and flour, which he had prepared. He was drinking a cup of linden tea.

I have a beautiful story to tell you, he began. As he spoke, Eva's brother B translated blow by blow, leaning into my ear. He needn't have, because Big A spoke slow and clear.

The story was this:

Very early in the morning, around 7 a.m., a retired fisherman was seen walking with his cane. He had a profound, melancholic look of longing. A woman stopped him – a person who had been neighbor and friend for a long time. She saw him walking towards the hospital, it seemed to her, whereas she usually sees him at the fish market.

She seemed to know the source of his sadness and started questioning him – are you going to visit someone special? Is is someone you have not seen forever? Did you miss her? When did you see her last?

The old fisherman shook his head to each pause between her questions. There was a lingering sadness about him, a *saudade.*

Where are you going, then?

The man who spent his life on the sea looked at her with a sense of deep nostalgia locked into the moisture of his eyes.

I am going to the market, he said, to take a long look at the fish.

July 11

I am recording this because I think it will help reveal how my irritation is meaningless and small-minded. This might allow me some perspective. Already, after formulating that sentence I am feeling more calm.

Last week, Eva's mother prepared an *alheira* (Jewish chorizo) in the oven for lunch – but because I was not in the house, and I had gone to Porto to lunch at a *tasco* recommended by Eva – her mother heated it up for dinner. I am noting how many times Eva and her family do things for me so that I may remind myself in the future that if I show ingratitude in any way I should be ashamed. Before Eva's mother reheated the *alheira*, she mentioned she was using the *microondas*, or microwave, and that she usually does not use it. I asked her if we shouldn't cut the metal key-ring that binds the ends of the *alheira* with a twine, because it would catch fire in the *microondas*. She agreed that it was probably best to remove it, so I cut off the metal ring, and she placed the *alheira* in the microwave and set the timer for two minutes. When it came out, it was hard as a brick, but I ate without complaint. It was still very tasty, and as a guest, I should always be polite.

Upon hearing this story, Eva became insistent (as did all her brothers) that mom would never heat an *alheira* in the microwave and they all ganged up on me to say that my remembrance of that day was false. This is a pet-peeve of mine, but I had to back down because I am a guest, and therefore any insistence on my version of events would be petty, small-minded and inappropriate. So I remained seething inside.

I recognize that however certain I am that I did not hallucinate (I was utterly sober whereas medications for painkillers were scattered on the table for her mom's toothache) I cannot defend for such a petty reason – and furthermore, that no one is judging me. Even more, I am not in a court of law where one must plead a case. People believe what they want to believe – but it would be better if I took a deep breath or just walk away before I even begin an argument.

Reminder: every day I spend in this house is a gift. Do not ruin it with your rotten ego.

July 11 (continued)

Burning of the Cat Under Investigation from Público [Seixta 3 JUL 2015: Prossegue Investigação da Queima do Gato]

There is a village which maintains a strange tradition: every year a cat placed in a basket, raised up high into the upper branches of a tree and set on fire. This article in Público was not about the animal cruelty angle of the burning of the cat ritual. The woman's complaint in this article was not out of a concern for the animal's safety. The villager's issue was one of envy. She did not find it fair that the same cat owner has the opportunity, year after year, to have her cat placed in the basket and singed by the tree fire. She wanted her cat to be included in the burning ritual. She wanted her cat to narrowly escape the fire, the hairs nearly entirely burned off her skin.

In a separate article, an 81-year old man from the same village was interviewed for his opinion about the tradition.

I can assure you, he said, no cat has ever died in the burning of the cat ritual. The cats walk away with their fur browned over, but they are never mortally wounded. They even used the same cat the last 3 or 4 times.

July 12

The Cleaning Lady and the Burning Cat

There is an element of daily life here that I have thus far failed to give proper space, at my own peril – and that is C, the cleaning lady. But first, I want to mention that last night Eva and I made cornbread and it was wonderful.

When I returned from a bike ride along the coastline (the ever-renewing seaside) she appeared on the staircase wearing only panties and a Madonna Blond Ambition t-shirt.

Now, about C – she is an exceptional person who manages dishes, ironing and general cleaning for the house, who is always polite but nonetheless every day causes one or another confusion. It took Eva's mom and dad forty-five minutes to track down where C had hidden the comforter and bedsheets for the bed downstairs in the livingroom.

There is a story there, by the way, about the spirits that live in that room at night, akin to the origin of the *Quinta das Chapadas* or *Ranch of the Slapping Ghosts* – in brief, this was a family house in Viseu, and every time someone from outside the family attempted to sleep, they would be plagued by the sensation of dozens of hands slapping them awake. As the story goes, these are family ancestors protecting their land. Similarly, the living room is no easy place to doze off.

C has a habit of placing clothes under the cabinet stairs once they are dry, for ironing, which results in a pile of everyone's clothes together under the cramped cupboard. Never wishing my clothes to be ironed but without the vocabulary to express it, I am always retrieving clothes (a sock here, but not there) but because I only have enough for a suitcase I am constantly out of clean socks and underwear. Thus, it becomes a game of finding my underpants or else washing them myself, as I did last night in the bathroom sink. I let them soak in the sink overnight because it was late and there was no room on the drying rack. In the morning they had disappeared. They were not on the drying rack outside – I asked C if she knew what happened. She said "I already washed them," led me to the back of the kitchen, and pointed to a red bin where there were several pairs of underwear soaking wet – but none of them were mine.

Onions In the Closet

When we returned to the house, Eva entered the kitchen to prepare herself some fried potatoes. Her staple diet is fried potatoes, hamburgers and fried eggs. She pours the olive oil into the deep-fry pan. She ignites the flame. She cuts the potatoes into even discs, and slips them two at a time into the bubbling oil.

Mom, she yells from the closet at the back of the kitchen. What are you planning to do with these onions? They're rotting, and I already told you that I get asthma if you cook with onions.

Her mother answers a semblance of denial from the livingroom.

I peek over the top of the box. Twelve onions, at least three of which are so grey they look like they died and returned as ghost onions. Overturned, the flies escape.

Take these to the garbage before she decides to cook them, Eva says. Put them in this plastic bag.

Should I really throw them out?

I don't know. You've seen what happens if she cooks them – I have to leave the house.

But what if she sees me?

Okay, forget it. Just cover them with this plastic.

Which plastic?

July 13

Almost a Construction Worker

I am in the kitchen, drinking coffee in the morning alone – nobody is yet awake. I have rolled up the shutters in the livingroom, not using any lights or electricity yet, conscious of how expensive the bills are at the now Chinese-owned utility.

Oh good, says Big A, you're not using the lights. They're charging the maximum possible per watt, these criminals – we paid nearly 350 euros last month for our light bill.

That's far too much, I say. They shouldn't be allowed to charge that.

You've really got quite the tan, says Big A. Do you have that underneath your shirt, too?

I lift my threads, exposing the bare white skin. Eva then appears on the stairs.

Your husband looks like a construction worker, says Big A, with that pale belly and tanned only on his arms and face.

The Kamikaze Kiss

Ants in the room. I woke up yesterday with one crawling on my upper arm tattoo, the one where Eva's name is written out in full – including all six of her names. Then, last night there was one skirting the wooden frame of the bed – in B's room, where I sleep now much of the time.

M, who is Eva's shortest friend, came to the house for lunch. Eva made hillbilly food, as she calls it, in her own way, with a coffee gravy. Beans and chorizo or *salpicão* instead of bacon – cornbread made from sweet yogurt and olive oil – a lactose free yogurt, a yogurt whose enzyme it was later discovered was the culprit for her red welts, those same red welts we thought might have been adult measles. After thirty days in Portugal I am beginning to lose my English prepositions. M tells stories – comedian style – I do not know if this style is intentional, but she seems like a professional comedian the way she pauses before a punchline – and this time, she talked about a guy who managed to actually chip her tooth with the clumsiness of his kissing technique. She called it a "kamikaze kiss," owing to its swiftness and destructiveness. Here is what happened: she had gone to an opening night at Ambos – a kind of gallery or what they call an "alternative space" and she was there with her ex-boyfriend. Now, there were two separate – but equally disturbing moments that night – the kamikaze kiss was not the first. M's ex-boyfriend was apparently still enamored with a skinny blond who was tip-toeing around an installation of what M described as a giant cotton swab – and he had engaged her in conversation with M just standing next to him, but not introducing or linking her in with the dialogue. He did, however, while reminiscing with the blond, unwrap a piece of bubble gum and hurl the gum violently into M's mouth. He and the blond continued reliving their memories as the began doing the same with chocolate candies – without looking, he would throw his hand over M's mouth and shove in a bon-bon. After the blond left, her ex swooped in for the "kamikaze kiss", knocking out a clump of chocolatey bubble gum, causing her lip to bleed, and flaking off the better part of her front tooth.

Reminder: write the story of the musician I know, a professional harpist who after an early music performance one night, in White Plains, stumbled on the ice, fell on her front and chipped her tooth, which was then removed. How she preferred her new look, and decided to keep it. How she wanted the cover for her new album to include the missing tooth in her smile.

July 14

Rooster Fish (Part One)

Do you know *galo*? Big A asked me in the kitchen. This is pre-coffee grogginess reporting. There is a plastic bag filled with fish in the sink.

You mean the olive oil?

He shows me the fish shaped like a triangle with a large head and gristle under its chin.

Cock. It is the fish cock.

A rooster fish?

Yes, this we call the fish cock.

Was it caught here in Foz?

No, this fish is from further north, Matosinhos. It is last night's catch, he says, holding the long, flat fish. It is still covered with patches of sand.

He hovers his nose over a divot under the fins, pokes it more open with a finger and inhales deeply.

Smell, he says, offering the fish to me.

I breathe with my snout directly in the hole. It does not smell like the freshest fish in the world – it smells like a breeze one might catch off the surf – like the freshest ocean air imaginable.

You know the North Pole? he says. Some of Portugal's ocean currents come from the North Pole which carries this fish. This one is called *linguado*, he says.

Do you know the English name for this fish?

Flounder, I think.

He picks up a smaller flounder – palm-sized.

Proibido, he says.

After experiencing the scent of the divine *linguado,* freshly caught, only now do I think I can begin to comprehend the very short tale which Big A told me last week.

There was a perfume to the *linguado* – no – these words are too crude to describe it. "Perfume" sounds fabricated, overly pungent. It was not a strong scent, but very distinct. It was more like the fish has acquired a method to distill the best smells of the sea and keep them inside that pocket just behind its gills. There, under that flappy skin was a frigid wind blown in from the North Pole.

Journal #2 (gold)

July 15

The Optometrist

I think that I am a problems-collector. If living with the same circumstances, another more average, less talented man would be happier.

My major talent — as I see it — is in creating and then compiling numerous minor issues which, before meddling, did not exist. Let's take my new glasses, for example. My old pair of glasses had the frames cracked, and the lenses would fall out. Clearly this was an issue — even so, much better than the problem I have now with the "new" glasses: dizziness, nausea, and headache should not be side-effects from wearing spectacles — at least, this should not continue for several days.

Here is what happened. There was a new optometrist that opened in Eva's neighborhood and they were offering discounts on new frames. At the bottom of the hill, next to the bright red telephone booth which overlooks the sea. The two women at the store seemed friendly enough and I found a frame that I liked, and Eva liked also. We put the glasses on hold.

A week later, I returned to pick them up. They ran my credit card through their machine. It was declined. I gave them a different card, which was also declined. We could try the old machine, one of them said, but last time it didn't work.

I wonder why it didn't work? the other one said.

I don't think we ever found out, said the first one.

It was then that they remembered this was a totally new machine for credit cards. They opened some drawers, grabbed some cables and connected the machine, which was until then free-floating and not associated with any network. It was as if we had been just pretending, or play-acting that a customer was making a purchase. After connecting the machine, they ran my cards once again. Both were denied. I told them I would grab a cash card from the house, and walked away with my broken lenses up the street. I stepped to the curb and the right lens fell out and landed on top of my shoe. I popped the lens back into the frames. There was a liberal schmear of shoe polish blurring my vision. I did not have the keys to the house, so I rang the buzzer. Big A opened the door. Wrong card, I told him, as I opened the door under the stairs to unravel where my clothes live.

I returned to the "Oculista." They ran my debit card – it was denied. This had not happened at other points of sale in Porto.

I think you need to fix your machine, I told them. They apologized.

The only option then was cash, since they did not know how to use either of their credit card machines. I left once again, and returned with the cash. They fit the glasses over my nose, and I looked around at the newly bent world.

You'll get used to the new glasses, they said.

But is the prescription correct? I felt woozy already, like a drunken architect. The floor was crisp and clear, just miles from my feet. I stumbled and caught my balance just outside their door.

That afternoon, we drove to Cerveira for the Biennale – Portugal's first. The town was old cobblestone and mostly white buildings and there were green hills and folktales about the witches that once lived on the Spanish side, which was on the opposite of a grey, dusty mountain. I began to feel dizzy, and with the perspective completely out of wack I had the sensation that my legs were disconnected from my brain. I did not see much of anything that afternoon because my head felt like a tigertooth shark jaw had latched its jaws onto my skull. I hung the glasses on the front of my t-shirt. The crowd was thickening and my spectacles got tangled with someone's glasses as we exchanged kisses. We could barely bring the glasses apart. Then, a man grabbed Eva's shoulder and yelled into her face, Drive! according to her account, but I did not see it. I did not see anything.

I must have seemed deranged, trying to dislodge the glasses from the front of her shirt with clumsy fingers, my unfocused eyes staring bluntly around – and everything I attempted to say in Portuguese came out inadvertently pornographic. In my enunciation of a phrase as simple *as pleasure to meet you,* I emphasized the sleaziest connotation of 'pleasure'. Explanations did little to conceal my handicap.

Eva noted my condition and brought me *empanadas* from the catered outdoor reception, which I could only imagine was gorgeously presented. I could smell the white wine, and it was not the acrid, vinegary concoction which passes for wine in most of the States. The *tortilha* was superb.

Later, we drove to a party in Vila Nova de Gaia – still with no lenses on and an immense headache. Nighttime as it was by then, I could see even less. When we arrived at the party – where it seemed that everyone was a sculptor – we gathered around a table packed with foods. Take whatever you like, Eva said, but I could not see what there was in front of me. Then, we went to the balcony, where I felt the wall with a strong grip so that I did not fall over the ledge onto the road below. It's a beautiful view, said the party's host, and I nodded. I could not distinguish land from sky or sea, but the lights were vivid and impressionable. I knew there was an ocean down below, and traffic not far off the sound of breaking waves. It is quite a vision, I said.

Dream About the Cleaning Lady

Eva's mother had a dream last night. In the dream, the cleaning lady arrived at early, at 7am, in order to tickle her.

Hello, said the cleaning lady, I've arrived a bit early to joke around.

Okay, said Eva's mom, then she started to tickle her.

In the dream, Eva's mother then asked the cleaning lady if she, too was ticklish.

Not at all, said the cleaning lady, not in any part of my body.

When she awoke from the dream, I was making coffee and the cleaning lady was in the kitchen, ironing Big A.'s shirts and trousers.

C, said Eva's mother, are you ticklish?

No, said C, I am not ticklish in the least.

Then, said Eva's mother, my dream was absolutely right.

Laundry in Reverse

D, says the cleaning lady as I am breakfasting on yogurt and cashews. Your laundry is on top of your suitcase.

Perfect, thanks, I say, and setting my spoon aside, I check the t-shirts which I had set to hang late the night before.

My attempt to do my own laundry usually does not backfire quite so badly, as the shirts are completely wet still, but folded neatly. I thank C for her work, and return to my yogurt. Eva's mother descends into the kitchen to tell C to have a good weekend. C is removing her apron and opening the door.

Thanks for your help, says Eva's mother as she shuts the door.

I rinse out my spoon in the sink, and return to my laundry. I unfold every t-shirt and place them back on the drying rack. I open the back door, and set the drying rack outside in the sun.

July 18

Mandela's Birthday

Today is a day where I do not speak, but only listen.

On this day was born a man who, having been condemned to prison for defending the rights of the people against apartheid harbored not a shred of hatred for his jailers when released after twenty-six years. What could I possibly have experienced that comes anywhere near that? *Fuggettaboutit.*

Down the hill, past the red phone booth to the ocean promenade. A group of cyclists rush behind me, a taxi nearly swipes me front side, a van follows swiftly behind again nearly not missing me. I meander the path northbound along the volcanic shoreline, pausing at the overlook with a statue of Camões.

Preoccupied now with questions I might be qualified to answer, for example: who is the most significant Portuguese writer in history – Luis de Camões or Christiano Ronaldo?

Onion Soup

Last night, Eva kicked me out of the bedroom at 4am. In her reckoning of things, when I went to the bathroom I did not fully close the door, and let a mosquito into the room. The mosquito began to bite her, first on the tips of the fingers, then on her upper arm, eventually munching on her eyeball. Her *eyeball*.

Get out, she said. You let wild animals into my room and now I'm bitten and it's your fault.

I retreated to the broken cushions in the livingroom.

In the morning, awakened by the distinct scent of raw onions, I knew there would be trouble. C, the cleaning lady was slicing white onions and boiling them for a French Onion soup.

Within a matter of seconds, Eva careened down the stairs and with flurry of heated words she was out the door.

I tried to pull my laces together in time to catch her on the street.

I'm sick of it, she said, as she wandered in sweatpants and tennis shoes in the direction of the ocean.

It's like the more that I say I get asthma from onions, the more they want to cook with it. There are a million things you can cook without onions, so why suddenly this renewed love affair with onions? says Eva. We are walking down the hill. At the end of the hill is the red telephone booth, and the ocean swelling with algae, depositing it onto the rocky shore.

Maybe, I say, it has to do with the allure of the prohibited.

Or maybe my mom just gets into her head to make my life completely miserable.

I don't know, sweetie.

Why can't they be obsessed with potatoes or califlower? Why does it have to be onions, onions, onions?

I don't know, sweetie.

I think I'm going to start smoking in my room.

Why?

Because then they would start to feel half of what I feel when they boil onions, Eva says.

I see.

Or I will do a bunch of spray paint in the livingroom, because last time I did that my father complained he could not breathe.

I'm not sure what the answer is.

But do you understand why they would do that to their daughter?

I don't know. Nobody's perfect.

Once or twice I would understand. But lately this is getting to be too much. I'm seeing this happen every other day.

I know.

What's the solution? How do I make people understand what I'm going through? Do I have to dump a bottle of bleach in their bedroom?

You wouldn't be able to breathe with that, either.

That's true. But it's no better now, is it? I have to leave and walk around aimlessly for who knows how long, Eva says, opening the accordion door of the telephone booth.

Get in, she says, but the booth is too small.

Sweetie, did you really get bitten on the eyeball?

She plants a kiss, and there is the sound of a splash nearby like someone poured out the contents of a soda on the sidewalk. There is no sign of anyone around, only a lone seagull which squaks as it hovers over the striped triangle tents on the beach.

July 19

Family Diagnosis and Rooster Fish (Part Two)

Terrible night – a headache debilitated me completely. I suspect the mini-bread I picked up at the neighborhood bakery was the culprit – because of my sensitivity to potassium sorbate, and now that some U.S. preservatives are making their way into the Portuguese food industry, foods are swelling with tasteless fillers like soy lecithin. And until yesterday I had never tried that particular type of bread. Accompanying the headache was a nausea that I could not shake – but the best part was how the whole family tried to diagnose my issue.

Eva said it was the cassava and fish that I ate yesterday. I disagreed, and everyone disagreed it could not have been the cassava as it is the most mild and inoffensive food on the planet.

You should not drink water, said Eva's brother A. It's bad for your liver.

Pull down your eyes so I can see the whites, said Eva, as she examined the color. Yup, said Eva, it's a yellowish color which means liver. You've had too much greasy food.

Stop the water, said her brother A.

Your liver can't handle the grease, said Big A. You should see a doctor. Did you eat anything greasy yesterday?

I did have a buttered toast at a *tasquinha*.

That's definitely the problem, said Big A.

I think it was the yogurt, said Eva's mother. What's the expiration date?

At this, the fishcock again appeared, and Eva's mother began grilling it right there in the kitchen. The smoke began rolling into the hall, then the livingroom, fogging its way up the stairs as Eva turned on the kitchen fan then disappeared. I retreated into the main sitting area. The smoke was so thick it looked like there was a fire in the house, and this was not good for my nausea. Eventually, I had to stand outside the door, smelling the fresh air to evade the amount of smoke.

But the night was even worse – I had the unstoppable sensation that I was gagging from deep down inside my gut, both Eva and I taking turns to switch on the kitchen vent only to have it turned off by Big A – and vice versa, we spent the entire night descending the stairs to switch on the fan, while only a few minutes later Big A would turn it off. The headache remained so powerful that every movement felt like a fireworks display inside my ears. But the best part was the next day, when Big A asked if I was feeling better – and I answered honestly, no – at that point, the diagnosis changed.

It must be jetlag, said Eva's brother A.

But I've been here for two months, I said.

Yes, it's definitely jetlag, he said.

I looked into the dictionary, I said, trying to sway the conversation into other territory. I have a migraine, which in Portuguese is called an *enxaqueca.*

It was at this moment that Eva walked into the room.

You said what?

I have a migraine.

Do you know what you just said in Portuguese?

I hope it wasn't offensive, I said, already preparing to be embarrassed again.

You said that you were stuffing your underwear – it only leaves us the question of what are you shoving into your underwear – French fries or olives or raw meat?

July 20-25

Amares, Green Wine Country

Notes for stories to write:

> Pissed off landladies
> Mystery Couple – Fake Marriage
> Mystery Party – finding a place to stay
> Silent Baby
> The Piscina vs. Football
> The Public Pool and Falling Lifeguards with Oranges
> Rifles and Pigs on The Olive Farm
> Dogs and Roosters are Not Noise
> Serial Killer D, Dream part one
> Tasteless Orange
> The Plum That Tasted Like a Flat Tomato
> The Pat on the Head (Pet Peeve)
> The Barber of Amares
> Asthma in the Countryside
> Swimming Pool with Insects
> The Sister-in-Law
> Museum of Dust
> Comedy at the Quarry
> The Camel's Drool and the Butcher
> The Smokehouse (*salpicão*, *presunto*, blood sausage)
> Bitten on the Eye by a Fly

Gathering Supplies (in search of the elusive breadknife: pizzeria, tasco, butcher, city hall)

Reminder: write the story of getting glasses "fixed" at the other more "reliable" *oculista:* how they force-bent my frames – how

the guys were painting the walls inside with a room full of customers – how Eva remained outside because of allergies to the
paint – how the guy (short with missing teeth) bounced my
lenses on the countertop to demonstrate their impermeability
– how the lenses were then scratched – how the white paint
splattered the countertop.

Eva is so precious in the things that she says:

If you love me, you would be pitching a tent with me all
the time and people would call you the pitching-a-tent man.
Where is it? she says. I want a tent.

My only comeback was weak: if you can't say it, then at
least blink if you love me.

July 26

The waves crash on the volcanic rock at Praia do Leme in the
North of Portugal.

Correction:
The waves do not crash. They are not that strong.

Reminder: do not mention "Alaskan Salmon" to E. Guaranteed conflict.

July 23

Amares, *Sexta-feira*

At the Sol do Minho vinho verde factory there were two op-
tions – the cheap booze or the expensive – we opted for the
same wine we had been drinking at the cantina in Amares – ten

Euros for a box of six bottles. This was the "expensive" one.
How did we find the place? We asked four times: first, a sweaty
bearded man with round arms and face beaten by the sun – he
was driving an official minivan of some kind and turned out
to be the Mayor of Amares.

You'll see an old stone house at the top of the hill, he said
– from there, just ask around.

Next, we asked a lone old lady walking on the road – her
hair was sun-bleached and one of her eyes was closed over
from a permanent condition, probably. She pointed up the
hill. Finally, we saw an open gate with a long, narrow road that
seemed to go one-way into a field of grapes. We drove a bit
past and asked some guys unloading a truck – one was wearing
an orange or green safety vest – do you know where the *vinho
verde* factory is? we asked. Right here, they said.

July 20

Arrival at Amares

We were looking for Mr. Guy, our contact. Where is Mr. Guy?
I asked Eva.

> Somewhere in the *largo* (plaza).
> Somewhere?
> Yes, she said. That is what he told me.
> He told you to meet him where?
> Somewhere.
> Yes, but where is the somewhere?
> Somewhere in the *largo*.
> Where in the *largo*? When?
> Today.

Did he give you a time?
He did not specify. He said to meet somewhere.
Somewhere?
Yes, that is the word he used.
When?
Sometime after lunch.
Those were his words? *Sometime?*
Yes.
That we are to meet him "somewhere, sometime after lunch?"
Yes. That's it.
I guess you have his phone number then.
No, I don't.

July 20

The Largo (Amares)

There was a church with a bell and a stone clock built into the wall. Blue tiles, like most. On the south side of the largo an inexpensive cafe where locals sat drinking beer. In the middle, a monument etched with the year 1940, with six names etched in the stone with tags, arrows, perhaps shields. The symbol of Portugal – castles, towers. The distinct feeling of ignorance passing through me. Of course, I was also wearing my new, fantastic pair of glasses which pretty much gave me vertigo.

We were standing in front of the monument when a girl appeared from behind us and tapped Eva on the shoulder.

Mr. Guy is here, she said.
Where? said Eva.
Here, near the largo. Somewhere.
Thank you for telling me.
The girl walked away.

We sat down at the bigger cafe next to the monument in the center of the largo. Eva, as usual, wanted nothing or else a popsicle to cool off with. Her brother A had a popsicle also, as usual. A's girlfriend T, the skinniest of us all, ordered a ham and cheese sandwich, an omelet, a chocolate croissant, a coffee, a juice, two beers and a cola popsicle. We watched as the waiter brought plate after plate and T devoured all of it, but when he brought her the popsicle, she said, could you first bring me a burger? And another beer?

We admired T's appetite, and the now midday sun.

Mr. Guy was nowhere.

We were talking about pet peeves. T's was being licked on the nostril. She said she really felt it was disgusting.

T was on her third beer when Mr. Guy showed. His jeans were almost dirty and he had a map of the village printed on a fancy brochure. There were logos printed on the bottom.

You are here, he said, pointing to a black rectangle on an orange background. The cantina is here, next to the technical school.

And the place we are sleeping? said Eva.

Somewhere close, he said. We are very close. When you are finished here, let me know and I will take you there, he said, looking over the remains of T's burger, omelet, sandwich, coffee, croissant and beers.

How will I find you? Eva asked.

I will probably be over there somewhere, he said, pointing to the cheap cafe south of the church.

You didn't need to bring anyone, said Mr. Guy to Eva. He peered over at me.

Eva said, what do you mean?

Because I'm the only slave you need. I will be over there somewhere, he said, pointing to the cafe south of the church.

He left, and Eva took my pen and wrote in the blank spaces of the pedals and rims of my bicycle tattoo: fuck me now.

August 1

I do not understand how it is possible when the cleaning lady returns my Ramones t-shirt it smells worse than before like moldy walls or the underside of some dog?

August 2

Free to Do What You Want

I think I have Stockholm Syndrome for my wife. Eva has a power over me like that of jailer and prisoner. Today, for example she tells me she wants to go to the movies. Bam! I'm in jail. We have to go to the movies. She wants me to drive – double whammo. That means I have to drive carefully, soberly, and avoid accidents – could there be anything worse? We get in the car. She walks extremely slowly in her condition – so much of what occurs healthwise to her is out of her reach – innate, genetic, inherited. Therefore she compensates by taking control. For example, when there is a television, she is the only person able to change channels – she tells me now "you are free to do what you want," but if I do change the channel she will walk outside into midnight streets and go back home. We are currently staying at the hotel in the neighborhood, a private getaway we take advantage of from time to time. Don't do that sound, please, she says, referring to my smacking lips or any other sound I make with nose or mouth. I've married a sexy dictator. And everything I see is still spinning around me from either a wrong prescription or maybe it's just the way things are now. Just a few minutes ago, while she was in the bath, I turned on the television. Instead of telling me to change the channel, she reached, dripping, into the back of the television and unplugged the cables. Then, she began to dress. After she finished dressing she left the hotel without a word. I followed her onto the street, begging her, like a good husband, to let me drive her to her house.

I won't leave you alone in the street, I said, not in the dark, not at night.

You are free to do what you want, she said.

She kept walking. I followed — or tried my best to follow, tripping over the concrete that seemed, in my perception, to be quite distant. And I would have followed her all the way home on foot. I told her this.

Go back to the hotel and watch your TV, she said. That's what I want you to do.

But, I retorted, you don't control me.

Her response was simple: Pull your pants down, and I'll go back to the room with you.

Here? I said. There was the old Foz castle behind us, and a Brazilian *Churrasco*, and a cafe, and a bar. An old man smoking outside in a tattered beige blazer had taken notice.

Right here, she said.

Okay, I said. I unlocked my belt. I let the jeans slide to my shoes. Now I know what to do in a crisis situation, I said. She smiled, she relented. I had passed the test.

Back in the room, she tuned into the Sci-Fi channel.

Eva, darling, why can't I also turn to a channel I want sometimes?

You are free to do what you want, Eva said, just not with me present.

So, earlier today was the same.

Drive me to the movies, she said, which I did. En route, I made the mistake to say I would like to stop at the hotel to get my phone and call back home quickly. I pulled onto the steep incline in front of the hotel.

You can't park there, she said. I don't want to go to the movies anymore. Take me home.

What?

Take me home or I'm walking home.

But I'll just be two minutes in the room, and right back.

Take me home, then leave the car there and me and my family will go to the movies.

Okay, Eva. That's what you want.

I started driving back in the direction of her house. We passed the Brazilian *Churrasco*, the castle, the old man smoking.

Then, she turned to me and said, I changed my mind. I want to go to the movies.

But Eva, you already changed your mind.

I want to go to the movies, now.

I made a U-turn and headed towards the theatre.

August 3

Ribeira Story

The clothes smell like sardines.

The upstairs neighbor is grilling, and she likes to throw the ashes over the balcony. Clouds of dust descend to the veranda where we hang our clothes.

I almost forgot to relate this to the journal – the other night, Eva's mother told us an incredible story about their old neighbor in Ribeira. This story is from the time when the family was living there before relocating to Foz. The neighbor was her good friend, she said — she would look over the kids when they were playing across the street. But she would come upstairs to chat with Eva's mom around lunchtime. These conversations took place in the hallway outside the apartment, with the door ajar, for hours.

They would talk each about their families and usually the neighbor would include some juicy bits of Riberia gossip. Then as if an alarm had gone off the neighbor would panic, and ask what time is it?

It's almost one p.m., says Eva's mother.

The neighbor would say, it's time for me to run to the window to curse at that rude construction worker.

What construction worker?

There's a worker who always urinates onto the street from the fourth floor of the next building. It's digusting. Someone has to stop him, the neighbor would say, and run back to her apartment.

Then, everyone could hear the neighbor yelling at the guy, Porco! Porco! And the worker would yell back — if you don't like it then stop looking! And the neighbor would scream again, Porco! Porco!

The next day, the same neighbor would come to gossip with Eva's mother again, and once more, just before one o'clock she would go yell Porco! at the construction worker. And he would return the favor.

This went on for a number of years, as the construction project was a long, drawn out affair. By the time the building was finished, the neighbor had married the construction worker, and they were renting an apartment in the very building that he had completed. Their apartment was on the fourth floor.

Fiascos, Plural

Then there was the fiasco of the hotel room — why was I in a hotel room again? Of course we had a disagreement — a miscommunication — I was driving Eva to an appointment in central Porto — and she gave me a knock on the back of my head so hard (a solid *cachaço*) I stopped the car in order to calm myself down. Calming her down is out of the question — it is akin to reasoning with a bull in the midst of a charge — language of any sort could be fatal. I would be wise to take her brother's advice: when Eva wants something, it's easier to give in than to resist, because such is the force she wills against any opposition. So I stopped the car and she left. Not being familiar with central Porto, and still wearing my fucked-up glasses, I got lost for forty-five minutes before I was able to find the Douro River and follow the coastline to Foz. Fed up, I took my things out from under the stairs, and walked to the hotel.

Her father, Big A, always being warm and tolerant, invited me to dinner with the family the following day. It was by telephone that the invitation came, and I was still alone in the hotel room. Anxious to smooth out any bad feelings, I accepted — but this was before the fiasco of the room.

I had gone to the gym, if it could even be called that — it was a smallish walk-in closet-like space at the bottom of a spiral staircase behind the hotel bar. I lifted a couple of barbells and sprinted for ten minutes on the treadmill, staring only at the stone walls. Then, I felt like a swim but there were no towels available poolside. Mistake number one: I decided to jump into the pool anyway, thinking that I might just drip dry in the sun.

The fiasco of the room went like this: when I returned half-wet from the pool, the handle on the door swung too far to the left. It appeared loose and broken. But first, there was another weird run-in with the concierge.

While swimming, I had felt again the weightlessness of the water and for a brief time all things of consequence left me and I had no more worries than keeping my body afloat, watching the contour of the two palm trees on each side of the pool. The conceirge was rearranging the deck furniture, but there was nobody else in the pool. This was sometime around 7:45pm, which puts anyone Portuguese (and Spanish tourists also, of which there was at least one family with a super loud crying baby, *ai meu deus*) either in preparation for, en route to, or in the middle of that all-consuming national ritual: dining. This was the same concierge who — on the eve of our first anniversary — had assumed at check-in that we would be paying by the hour.

Therefore, I was alone in the pool, but the concierge was always looking in my direction. Maybe I had something on my face — maybe the dark spots had grown much worse than I realized around my temples — maybe they were highly visible — maybe he knew someone who died only a few short months after developing spots such as mine. I hope not, but if I croak from some disease I want it to be fast. Eva is always worried about my spots.

But the concierge would move an ashtray stand, then a lounge chair, then another ashtray stand, fluffing a pillow on the sofa, then he would look over at my spots. He completed the arrangements of the furniture under one of the palm trees, and keeping his eye on me, moved around the chairs under the other palm tree. Was he concerned about my being alone in the pool that I might not have anyone to rescue me if I drowned? Why was he staring? Had he never seen an American with tattoos before? Maybe that was it. He was staring at my bicycle tattoos — the Centurion on my shoulder, the Schwinn around my nipples", the classic velocipede across my shoulder blades.

After he left, I decided it was time to drip dry and get a shower before dinner. The walk to the house would take twenty minutes, which left me enough time for a shower and change. I dried off with a tiny towel I had rescued from the gym, but my shorts were still dripping when I caught the elevator. The handle on the door when I returned to the room was so jammed it appeared to have been reinstalled upside down. All the other doors had handles perpendicular at rest. This handle was at a very odd angle indeed. The door would not open, and the light stayed green. The light was to signal the clear opening of the door, posted above the handle. I moved the handle around at all angles. It felt like it had been generously lubricated at the joint. I panicked. I thought somebody might have broken the lock to get inside then jammed it so it would not open, or maybe the thief was inside now, holding back the door. I waited around the corner for a minute to see if anyone would exit my room. The motion detector light went off, then I jerked my knee and it came on again, lighting the hallway of the third floor. I watched the door of my hotel room. The light again extinguished itself, and nobody came in or out. Still dripping from my shorts, I removed myself to the elevator.

At the front desk, I explained to the receptionist — a boy I had never seen before — that I could not enter the room. He accompanied me to the third floor. He could not open the door. I watched as he mimicked the same motions I had just explained to him in my broken Portuguese. He called the concierge. He argued with him while pushing and pulling on the door, moving the handle up, down, left, right, pushing above the lock while pulling on the handle, all the while screaming with the phone between his shoulder and ear. The light in the hallway was motioning on and off. Above the handle the light was green, and he inserted the card and tugged again on the door. The concierge on the phone asked him if he tried moving the handle in all directions. Yes, he said, I tried pulling to the left, to the right, up and down. Is the light green? said the concierge's voice. Yes, the light is always green, he said. The boy kicked the door with his foot, then he knocked on the hinges with his knuckles.

The concierge said, did you try kicking the door?

Reminder: do not mention "tea" in conjunction with the word "caffeine" to E. She will become hostile.

All told, it must have taken twenty minutes for the boy to pry open the door. Of course, by then I wanted to change rooms, which would make me late for my dinner appointment. After packing my things, the front desk neglected to call me with my new room number – so I ventured to the elevator, which was jammed with Spanish tourists. At the front desk was a series of puddles left by some unconsiderate guest. It was twenty more minutes to get a new room – I gave the boy Eva's father's number and told him to call and explain why I would be late for dinner.

On checkout, the concierge was again up front. But when I approached, he seemed to have forgotten I was already checked in. How many hours? he said.

There is Only One

Daddy, I want to poop now, says Eva as she enters the kitchen, pouting and upset.

Try eating bananas and prunes – how do you say prunes in Portuguese?

Ameixas, says Big A.

But I have been wanting to poop for three days, she says.

Big A. turns to me and says — Eva is unique in all of the world — there is only one Eva.

August 4

Finally, Some Sleep

Amazed I was able to sleep last night without waking up more than three or four times pressed up tight against the wall. By sleeping belly up with my arms crossed like Dracula in a coffin, I was almost relaxed enough to sleep most of the way through. This morning, I stretched out in the narrow space between the long couch and the footrests – I almost managed to feel human.

Reminder that all relationships have issues – the only ones that don't are a complete fabrication on film. Decisions to stay or go can only be based on the relative difficulty of whether or not we want the problems we currently have. For me, I like these problems. These are – taking the long view of things – managable problems, entertaining problems, wonderful problems to have. If I can manage to survive sleeping this way with Eva, I will do my best to adjust to this life. Being without her is not an option.

August 6

The Possibility of a Child

At the cafe today, the one with the statue of Ganesh, Eva brings up the subject of pregnancy.

I want to ask you a question about kids, she says.

Okay – ask me.

Given the advancement of new technologies, Eva says, would you be willing to carry a child to term?

What do you mean, carry the child?

I mean, Eva says, would you do a male pregnancy if you could?

Is that really a thing?

I think it is a thing, she says – or if it's not a thing it's about to be a thing.

Let me understand what you're saying – you'd want me to be the pregnant one? As in, a man with a baby?

It's a question, Eva says.

Are scientists looking into this? I mean, how?

I think they're doing studies.

What kind of studies?

Men with babies kind of studies. So, would you entertain the possibility?

I doubt you would like the way my body would change.

Now, isn't that interesting, she says.

Considering how superficial you are – you admit that you like a man with muscles and a flat belly.

But isn't that interesting you would worry about how you look.

Well, with all those hormones and an expanding belly, I think I would lose the hard body.

Because that's what I said the other day – that if I were to get pregnant, Eva says, I worry that you wouldn't like my body anymore.

But that's different, I say. I'm sure you would be gorgeous.

How is it different? The only difference is that you're a man.

But where would the baby go – supposing this were really a thing?

Somewhere between the stomach and the intestines, probably.

Probably?

That's more or less where it goes in a woman's body.

Except women have a uterus.

Maybe they implant a fake uterus inside the man, says Eva. Maybe that's how it works.

I have no idea. But I've made up my mind – the answer is no.

No – what ?

The answer is no. I would not want to carry a baby to term.

So why would you think that it's different for women?

Maybe it's biological? Isn't there some kind of maternal instinct, or evolutionary psychology behind it?

Yeah right, says Eva. Like I have an instinct to lose my hips and create stretchmarks forever. Hell no – I like my body the way it is now.

August 7

More Underwear Problems

Why did my mom put my underwear next to the codfish? Eva says. Now my underwear will smell like codfish. I have to wash them again.

Eva is removing her underwear from the back kitchen into a red plastic bowl. She takes the bowl into the lower bathroom, where she sprays them with the showerhead.

This is the third time I have to wash my underwear, says Eva. The first time they cooked onions, so my underwear smelled like onions, which gives me a huge allergy. The second time, they boiled tomatoes and set the pot of tomatoes next to my underwear. Now, it's the codfish. Why doesn't anyone let me do my laundry?

Why are you hanging your underwear in the kitchen?

Because anywhere else and they will move it around, or if it's outside the neighbor's dog hairs will land on it.

I don't know what's worse for your underwear – the smell of codfish or the scent of dog.

August 8

Cozido á Portuguesa

The morning's events are enough to fill the rest of this note-book. I will try to summarize it here, focusing most notably on Eva and her father Big A, and the interactions and discussions, arguments and squabbles – in preparation for and in driving to – the Cozido á Portuguesa restaurant in their old neighborhood, near Bolhão, where Eva grew up until the age of 12. First off, it is impossible to expect Eva to leave her bed before the hour of 1pm. If by some miracle, she wakes up to use the bathroom, she usually returns to bed and sleeps until 2 or 230pm. This, she explains to me, is because her doctor said that she has the lowest blood pressure of any human being in recorded history – and that she should be constantly in a sleeping or unconscious state when awake – and because of her unusually low blood pressure she requires 14 hours sleep daily to be properly rested.

The more serious problem however, is that Eva is unable to eat spicy or hard to digest foods as it could trigger an asthma attack, and *Cozido á Portuguesa*, it should be said, is notoriously hard to digest – a smoked meat lovers' delight made from boiling smoked meats like black pig chorizo, *salpicão*, veal, and an assortment of other chorizos and bacons and hams along with the occasional tongue, ear, and feet.

But first – the process of leaving the house. This process is not to be underestimated in complexity and time investment required to sufficiently move several bodies into the automobile, in this case A's black four-door sedan. The problem on this particular day was furthered by the fact that Big A's reservation for 1pm was already made impossible to meet because it was only at 12:45pm that he and the brothers began making the call for everyone to embark. "Everyone" is mom, dad, brothers, myself and Eva. The other thing was that both Z and T were to meet us at the restaurant and we had to pick up grandmother first in Ribeira – making a 1 pm arrival unlikely – but this is a typical day. Eva – having been awakened by her brothers – began hollering at them to let her sleep, and the brothers were yelling back. For my part, I was sitting in the living room, silent, trying not to make any quick moves. Eva says she does not want to go, but pressure from her father and brothers (also should mention it is her mother's birthday, her favorite spot) is high. She does not want to drive really far across town to not eat anything when she has diarrhea already. Their squabbles begin something like this:

Brothers – we're waiting for you, Eva.
Eva – go without me, then. I don't want to go.
Brothers – you're selfish. We are all waiting on you.
Eva – leave me here to sleep. Don't want to go anymore.
Father – we need to go. Brothers, let's go pick up grandmother.

Brothers – let mom pick up grandmother in her own car while we stay here and wait for Eva.

Eva – you don't need to wait. I already told you to go without me.

Father – it's already 1 o'clock. We're late for the reservation and we haven't even left.

The fracas continues in the car.

Walking towards the restaurant, Eva tours me around the neighborhood streets.

She says, I used to live in that building there on the fifth floor. I would shout across the street to the boy, Want to play doctor? I had a doctor's kit with all the working parts – stethoscope and all, plastic pills.

Did you know that playing doctor is a euphemism in the US?

For us it really means we play doctor. I take your pulse, check your lungs, and all that.

You had plastic pills? For kids?

My mom replaced them with candy so we could "take medicine."

I can't believe they would manufacture plastic pills so kids could choke on them.

That's my country, she says.

The pills were how big?

Small, like real medicine.

So kids were probably swallowing that all the time.

"Um cidade com tomatoes" was the poster inside the restaurant on the wall. Translation: a city with a real set of balls. This poster, an advertisement for Porto tourism, I think, replaced the Mother Mary that used to hang there when Eva was a child.

August 9

Tomato Jam

Eva's mother had bought a dozen "bull's hearts" tomatoes and they sat upside down in plastic crates until they began to collect flies in the widened craters at the bottom of the fruit. When we returned from the oceanside cafe, her mom was peeling the tomatoes, chopping the pulp and boiling them in her largest pot. This caused Eva to have an instant allergic reaction. Her face reddened as a beet. She said that it was so itchy in the unreachable nethers under her skin, she had the distinct sensation that relief could come only through tearing her nose off and scratching the fascia with a steel bristle.

We left the house, hoping the smell would disappear with the kitchen fan pumped on level three. Eva spent the night vomiting blood, and mused aloud that she would spray paint the living room if they boil more tomatoes.

The following day her mom continued boiling the tomatoes but set the pot on the back veranda to air. That pot of tomatoes remained there in the rain for 72 hours, as various conversations and arguments renewed and revolved in the house over the importance of continuing its boiling for another few hours. Her mom professed that the tomatoes required another six to eight hours of treatment on the stove. Eventually, the day came when I had to drive Eva to an academic appointment at the University. I waited in the cafe playing solitaire for an hour until the place filled with laborers eating the menu of the day, codfish (with potatoes, eggs and cilantro) for three Euros each. Someone by the pastries kept referring to me as a Frenchman, convinced perhaps because of my striped shirt and glasses or some vestige implicated in my dark jacket. I tried to ignore the comments, opened the door to the kitchen by mistake then entered the men's room. I paid for my sixty-five cent coffee and left. I waited at the rainy entrance to the building where faculty emerged to ash their cigarettes on my leather, and a freak wind picked up the other half of a Marlboro and projected it onto my jeans. Nobody noticed when I flicked it off, smearing the ash. Finally, after pacing the entirety of the yard and getting to know all the cracks on the lobby bench, Eva appeared ascending the long driveway from the center building.

Fuckers don't understand anything about my sculptures, she said.

We drove back to the house and found the pot of tomatoes filled with water rested on the countertop.

Can you take this to the tub? said Eva.
Why would I go all the way upstairs? I said.
No, she said, the tub downstairs here.
There isn't a tub downstairs. You mean the shower?
We call that a tub.
It's not a tub. It's a shower.
Whatever – can you take it there?
But it's full of water. It will spill.
I believe in you, Eva said.

And so I took the pot through the maze of carpets, umbrellas, newspapers and plastic bags in the hallway into the bathroom. I placed the pot – which still had a few peels of stray tomatoes – on the shower bottom and closed the curtain.

Then, her brother A came home. He went into the bathroom, failed to see the pot and put his foot directly inside.

August 10

Story I Told Eva Today About Almost Nothing

It's an office story. It takes place in New York – midtown Manhattan, not far from the Chrysler Building. The secretary in the office, a woman in her early sixties who had been working in the office for thirty years or more, one day announced she was leaving. But it was not through her, only via the Bureau Chief that news of her departure reached her coworkers. The Bureau Chief announced that a cash envelope would be assembled in the treasurer's office, and that everyone was invited to contribute any amount to that fund. He stressed that the donations were entirely voluntary. He did not mention the reason for the cash donations, only that they were to be her departing gift.

There were a couple of rumors, not very original, surrounding her departure – one that she was a secret scholar of Melville, evidenced by her constant references to Ahab and the known fact that she abandoned her passion for literature in order to take the job in the 1980's. That the thirty years in the office dried up her passion. That she was now packing a rucksack to wander South America with a notebook, presumably to die penniless but finally happy. Another that she had a wealthy suitor to fund a trip to places she had never been before, like the Caribbean, Paris, Pittsburgh. That she had saved nearly every penny, nickel and dime, and would retire in a scant cabana in Mexico. That she was a robotics expert, but no one had ever taken her seriously as she was a woman, and a recent robotics conference had reawakened her true calling. That she was a programming wizard who had hacked into a government server and was now on the run, and the cash had to necessarily be off the books. That she had been sexually harassed, and the cash was an attempt at settling the matter without bringing the accused to light, saving her from reliving the unpleasantness.

Instead, the Bureau Chief announced there was to be a secret party, disguised as a New Year's party in order to give her a send off – she was timid or extremely humble, he explained, and did not want anyone to notice her leaving. But the New Year's conceit was ill-disguised, as it was mid-September, and the Chief wasn't referring to Rosh Hashanah. A few days before the would-be party, the Bureau Chief sent another memo. The secretary had caught on and sabotaged the party efforts by leaving before the party date, and so it was announced by the Bureau Chief that if the coworkers wanted to see her off, it would have to be at 4:30 pm on that very day. When 4:25 pm came around, the coworkers gathered silently around the secretary's desk, with the Bureau Chief standing cross-armed nearby. The secretary said nothing, only noting that an awkward crowd was beginning to form around her as she packed her bag like a fugitive. She clicked off her computer and it made a final sound. She thanked everyone and went out the door. The coworkers returned – still silent – to their desks.

Within minutes, they received another memo from the secretary. The memo said just about nothing. Thank you for being so nice to me for the last thirty years, it said. I am very lucky to have worked with you all for so long. I wish you the best in everything that you do.

The mystery remained unsolved. Nobody seemed to know why she left, nor why she left so quickly, inexplicitly. The coworkers were lost. But about a week later another memo arrived. In this memo, the former secretary made another attempt, seemingly, to explain her departure. But the follow-up was a reiteration of the same platitudes, and told nothing of her reasoning, her whereabouts, or her thoughts or feelings on just about anything. She would have imparted more by sending a sketch and a signature, or a piece of bark from an area tree. It was, much like the first, fascinating in its void of meaning:

Dear colleagues, I am sorry that I left the office so suddenly, without explanation. It was truly humbling to be able to work with you for the last thirty years. Whatever you do, wherever you go in the future, I truly wish you the best. Happy New Year.

August 13

Showers, in Sickness and Health

Who took a shower? says Big A. It's about 9pm, close but not quite yet household dinnertime.

Oh you know, says Eva's mother, Eva makes D take a million showers a day.

It was in fact, the third shower I had taken — and not to be the last.

We had gone to the beach, and I had made the mistake of applying sunscreen on my arms, neck and ears. This sunscreen was not Eva-approved, which means it may or may not give her an allergy. As it happens, she asked me to stay at least one meter apart as we walked to the *praia*. Then, at the beach, the ice cold water proved ineffectual in relieving the scent. She kept her distance from the dogs without their owners on leash. In the water, on the sand, on the stone benches as we changed our sandy feet into sandals, on the walk back home, she kept her distance. Strangers with their kids passed her more closely than I.

On my third shower I took my time and used a fair amount of soap — a soap especially reserved for her without any fragrance, a soap which they call monkey soap because it smells like a monkey's armpits — consisting as it does of little more than animal fat. I use this same Eva-approved soap exclusively, for all purposes, in order that no fragrances touch my body or face at any moment. But the sunscreen had broken a sacred pact that I share with Eva — not to contaminate my body with foreign smells.

Now with my fresh towel about my neck, I approached Eva's bedroom door with extra caution. At this juncture there were two possibilities: I could either be approved as clear of the smell — an unlikely scenario — or I could be sent back for another rinse. This had happened many times. I knocked lightly, knowingly, on the door. Apprehension is my only constant.

What? says Eva.

I've come for inspection.

The door cracks open, and Eva emerges wearing her Blond Ambition Tour t-shirt and sunglasses. She begins sniffing at my shoulders, then moves to the neck and steps back.

No, she says. You're not entering my room like that.

And the door closes behind her.

So what do I do now? I say, knowing full well.

Try another shower, she says, until the smell goes away.

The soap had by now diminished to a nub the size of a snail. I rubbed up a lather with that snail so fierce that it made the skin behind my ears utterly flat and opaque and dry. I scrubbed the same areas now for the fourth time, with focus and intensity. I rubbed off the last of the soap from my shoulders, pressing all of my upper body strength against my own skin. I took extra care with the rinse. First, I rinsed off all the soap until my skin became rough — running a thumb over my clavicle to check there was absolutely no oiliness. I had covered every centimeter, every nook, every dip in musculature. With the second rinse, I used colder water and remained still a few minutes to air-dry – considering the probability that sunscreen had embedded itself into the towel. If there is anything I have learned in living with Eva, it is that contaminants are ever-present. Millions of organisms pestered our skin, feeding off our biology in a delicate symbiosis of which most of us are scarcely aware. We are a living ecosystem for billions.

The towel on my waist this time, I made the long and fateful climb to Eva's door. The inspection lasted longer this time. She lingered, inhaling a mole on my chin, and again a divot on the side of my neck, then back to the mole. These two spots were problematic.

Back to the car wash, she says.

But it's just those two spots?

Yes, says Eva, but soap them really well.

Then you'll let me in?

It depends on the quality of your work.

I returned to the bathroom and scrubbed in the sink. I dabbed with the towel, and knocked again, the towel draped off my shoulder and my body else wise bare.

The door cracked for a moment, then shut. I could hear her sigh from the other side.

It's the towel, she says. The towel has contaminated you.

But there isn't another towel I can use.

You're going to have to shower again, she says.

But how do you expect me to dry without a towel?

Figure it out. Use a t-shirt. I don't know. Just don't come in here smelling like that – you'll give me asthma.

And so it was that I came to shower for a fifth time. And on this occasion, I thought to perform a complete air-dry.

I stood waiting outside her door, not wearing the towel, not wearing anything – there was a breeze in the hall. I was shivering. I could only hope that nobody in the house would pass by and see me.

I knocked on her door and – success – she pulled me into the room.

August 23

Another Sunday with Grandma (Part One)

Mom, the chicken looks green, says Eva as she enters the kitchen.

It's fine, Eva's mother says. It's only the skin that's green.

But it smells funny – are you sure it's good to eat?

Of course, says her mom, placing the bird in a deep metal pan. She squirts a clear liquid over it with a baster, turns the bottom knob on the oven. The oven begins to make a whining sound, like a car engine that won't start.

I don't know if this chicken will make me sick, says Eva, and retreats upstairs to her room.

Eva's mother turns her attention to me and says, D, do you mind driving to go pick up grandma?

I don't mind.

Are you sure?

Yes, it's no problem. Do you need help with lunch?

Not at all. I will let you know when we go to pick up grandma.

I take a short rest on the sofa, awaiting her signal to fetch the car keys. Instead, I drift off asleep, only to awaken when my left leg is completely numb, circulation destroyed on the tough wooden edge of the worn seat. I enter the kitchen again.

Should I get ready to go? I ask.

But her mom says, Oh no – not for another hour or two. It's way too early for lunch.

I look up at the clock above the kitchen door – it's two o'clock in the afternoon. Internally, I know this will probably create a conflict because Eva had planned for us to go to the beach when she wakes up, which will be any minute.

Meanwhile, I busy myself recalling the laundry situation – Big A had asked me about a pair of pants I left wet in the lower bathroom. This, I realize, was a mistake. I had spilled some olive oil on its crotch, then inundated it with soap in order that the stain would resolve overnight. But Big A had removed the pants, and put them in a white plastic tub so that – as he now says – the cleaning lady will take care of it tomorrow.

Remembering this, I remove the pants from the back of the kitchen, and applying rigorous friction I rinse and hang it next to my other clothes on the back veranda.

Eva wakes up and tells me that we are going to the sand – that I must be ready with towels and sandals in five minutes or she will be leaving without me. Intimidating ultimatum.

Eva and I arrive at the beach, and we change into sandals on the concrete wall overlooking the shore below. We walk down the ramp, set our bags and towels in among the beach-goers and lifeguard, whose rope is set down on the sand to delineate the rescue area.

The waves are too strong, she says, as we venture into the ice cold water.

This is a magnificent problem to have.

After the swim, in which we are only able to stay in the water for a few seconds, we walk slowly back to the house. Along the beach path, a small boy comes running at me with an amateur fist half closed and throws a badly placed punch three fingers above my crotch. Lucky for me, he is too young to know where to aim or how to execute the hit.

Eva snaps at the father – you should control your child, she says.

Personally, I am too stunned to say or do anything. I do however, look down at my pants. There is a weird pattern of grease stained there, as if the kid had dipped his hand in butter.

As if I needed one more oily stain on my crotch.

Grandma and Gogol

When we return to the house, grandma is lamenting over a lost jacket.

I can only think of Gogol's *Overcoat*, as dull as I am with my understanding of the details in this most deceptively difficult Latin-based tongue.

I have the wrong jacket, says grandma, and I don't know whose this is.

But where did you get the jacket? says Eva's mother.

I don't know, but I know it's not mine. Where is my jacket? says grandma.

How would I know, mom?

This is a size 42 – I don't have anything that size. It feels like I'm wearing a curtain.

But didn't you bring it from your house?

Yes, this morning.

But it's not yours?

I've never seen this jacket before, grandma says. My jacket isn't wool, it's silk.

Just then, the phone rings – it's her son, Uncle J. We solved the mystery of the jacket, says Uncle J, who is broadcasting on speakerphone throughout the house.

What happened? says Eva's mother into the receiver.

Yesterday, says Uncle J, we went to Minho to visit the vineyard. I think that when we left the *quinta* she took someone else's jacket instead of her own jacket. As we were leaving, I took the jacket from her hands and put it in the trunk of the car. But the jacket – which was not her jacket anyway – was forgotten, and stayed in the trunk of my car overnight.

So how did she come to bring the wrong jacket today? says Eva's mom.

I returned to her house this morning, says Uncle J, because she called me continuously last night complaining about her missing jacket, saying that she left her silk jacket in my car. But when I brought her the jacket left in the trunk, she told me that she didn't recognize it. But – and this is the kicker – I'm not even sure she brought a jacket to the vineyard in the first place. I asked her, mom, are you sure you brought a jacket to the vineyard? And she said, I don't know.

So what you're saying, says Eva's mother, is that she took someone's jacket from a vineyard.

Possibly, says Uncle J, by accident.

I didn't steal anyone's jacket, says grandma.

Now, the mystery is partially solved, he says.

So what happened? says Eva's mother.

We just found her missing jacket on the floor of the closet.

The silk jacket? *Her* silk jacket?

Yes.

How did it end up there?

We think that it slipped the hanger and wound up on the floor.

115

It had never left the house.

That's correct.

The reason the mystery is still partially unsolved, says Uncle J, is because we don't know who is the owner of the wool jacket.

But this story does not end with the phone call from Uncle J. Despite inquiries to everyone at the *quinta*, the jacket's owner was nowhere to be found.

Not two or three nights afterwards, we had a dinner party at the house. Big A prepared a feast, with Eva and her mother presenting two different desserts, a heavily-liquored Port wine tiramisu and a *pão-de-ló*. At the end of the night, the guests took their leave and we spent our typical forty-five minutes saying our goodbyes in the foyer.

We shared a cup of linden tea around midnight. It was then that Eva's mother noticed that the wool jacket was missing.

August 27

Better than dreaming up any story, today is watching the waves roll into Foz

August 28

Driver's Legs

I wake up with a cramp in my right leg, and Eva moves off the mattress right away.

Maybe a coffee will help you, or a banana, she says, as I limp into the hall.

I have no idea.

You need to drive me to the University by 9am, says Eva. I have a meeting.

Okay, I will try to straighten out my leg.

We pull up into the parking lot at 945am, having been stuck behind a van loading children for nearly 15 minutes. Eva jumps out of the car, and says that she will meet me here when she calls. She hands me a cell phone.

Okay, what time will that be? I say, but she is already gone. My leg feels like an overused rubber band.

To pass the time, I decide to stay inside the car and read Camões. I have a terrible translation of the Sonnets, and try my hand at a re-translation of a sonnet that reads a lot like a verse from Lao Tsu's classic text *Tao Te Ching*:

Sonnet XLVII

Not only trends change but the times also change
lifestyles, friends, trust and its very foundations change;
reality is composed entirely of flux
steady only in its modification

Every visible phenomena appears as new
a misreading of our own preconceptions
the consistency of the malicious in our mourning
and my goodness is to be found only in memory

Time blankets the world with irreverent green
nestling up from yesterday's cracked ice
transforming the sweetness of spring into longing
embattled and frail the daily trials
of sorrow compounded from the realization
that change itself is not what it used to be

Eva's Dream

A guy was palming me, she said, then I ran away but the hand stayed glued to my behind. I looked around to find whose hand it was that apparently stretched out like a long rubber hose. It was a white guy in white pants.

From across the room, he said, so what?

I said, You can't do that.

He said, so what?

D's Dream

Driving: my leg was jammed stiff trying to stop the forward motion — we were glued to the vehicle in front of us — there were no brakes on the car. The only possibility was to use my heels to halt the momentum with friction from the soles of my shoes — which miraculously reached under the chassis of the automobile. I could feel the heat in my toes and smoke rolled off of my shoes but they did not break open. The car kept rolling, stuck to the other car's bumper. We halted in front of an old statue of the Flintstones in their family car. My only companion was a thin old man who resembled Barney Fife.

Dec 28

The Madrid I Never Saw

I have a talent for creating my own hell.

I had this idea to write a novel about the Madrid I Never Saw, because when in the Madrid airport, I typically have a 10 or 11 hour layover, overnight — too short to catch a train or bus into the city at midnight (to do what?) and too long for a comfortable layover – that this airport traps me inside and does not allow me to see the city itself – I get lost in the immensity of lights posed to face solar panels in the 100-foot ceilings, the futuristic steel beams painted acrid white, yawning arches hovering above the baggage check – even tonight, when I purposely reserved a hotel not far from the airport, I can feel that the airport wants to keep me stranded here, perpetually waiting for my flight to New York. Madrid is my Godot.

I sit down to write instead of calling the hotel for a free shuttle. I have this feeling of aversion, and would rather write. I do not wish to repeat the experience I've already had at this hour, waiting forty-five minutes for a city bus that did not appear. Or maybe, in some way, I crave the delirium of insomnia as a way to call upon the muse. Regardless if my reservation can be cancelled or not, I am less motivated to take my shoulder bag and change of clothes outside to the shuttle area than to sit at this lively airport arrivals area cafe at Terminal 4. I already took a shuttle to get here from my terminal of origin on the Porto to Madrid flight. Would the logistics of calling the hotel shuttle disturb the flow of my journaling? Undoubtedly.

But my goal is not to relate what happened over Christmas or how we didn't argue at all – we did – or how I found that my feelings for Eva are durable – they are – or how I was testing my Christmas experience as to see whether we should take different paths or not. As terrible and disturbing were the last few weeks with Eva, constantly bickering and lacking sex or any kind of enjoyment whatsoever together – it is not my goal at this moment to discuss. The point just now is to see whether I can still write. Word does seem to follow word in meaningful ways, and without effort or much thought. The way I first wrote when I wrote anything was this, a style of journaling without thought as to revision. For many years I rebelled against the impulse to write this way, but when I do extensive revisions the essence of truthfulness that emerges is not easy to achieve, so this time I will keep it as such – bare. With the fictions, they are fictions, but this *merde* is all true for the most part. No, I can't imagine being at a hotel is better than the Terminal 4 arrivals cafe.

There is a group of Russians sitting at a high table telling fables – a young, bald Russian brandishing a belt buckle in his hands, turning it over as the sisters or wives are all laughing loudly and proudly at the butt of some probably lewd jokes. Here the circular lamps stretch well into the ends of the hallways. Should I see about the shuttle? Maybe I could learn some Spanish from the hotel TV or maybe instead I should pull one off in the bathroom before catching my flight. Did I just say that?

Sometimes – and this is one of those times – with irrational behavior comes joy. This, I suspect, is because of the element of choice. I have chosen of my own free will to remain in the airport, despite the likelihood I will be charged for the hotel reservation and despite the sound logic of getting a few decent hours of shut-eye before an international flight – that is, assuming that the bus would actually arrive and take me to my destination. Instead, I opted for the irrational – less sleep, more discomfort and potential spiritual and/or physical degradation. It makes no sound sense and yet I am following this impulse, this nonsensical need. This happens to feel good. The rational – no, the sensible choice – that may be it more than anything – the idea that what makes sense for the comfort and ease of living, and usually this is tied in with convenience – the sensible thing to do would be to sleep a few hours in a nearby hotel, such as the one I had reserved. But I am thinking that more than the thrill of usurping the sensible is the possibility that the hotel I reserved is entirely wonky, some overrated rat hole with twelve euro drinks and a dysfunctional keycard that I would best avoid. But now at 00:42 hours, a certain fatigue is beginning to show its force. My watch, set to New York local time – is set to 6:42 pm – which makes going to sleep, on second thought less rational. Sleep, then, is inevitable.

Yet another point of rumination is my current indigestion. It started two days ago, just after Christmas dinner at grandmother's house. We decided that probably it was the turkey – although I had no idea at the moment of consumption that it was store-bought and undercooked. Each of the brothers had experienced immediate reflux upon bringing the dark, tender, red-lined meat to their lips, despite rumors that the turkey had been cooked for a few additional hours after the cousins procured it from the shelves of the *supermercado*. These points of heresay are contentious. But the true source of my digestive rumbling and eventual discharge – was probably the *recheio* – stuffing – which consisted of a very flavorful, chorizo-like, red meat and innards ground and stuffed into the cavity of the hungered bird – alas, its blood and organs were not fully recharged to settle intelligently in my lower intestines and thus have been calling me to service at 2-hour intervals.

Chime, chime, chime – passengers are asked to be at their boarding gate at the designated time.

Time only exists when we are counting. But there it is again – the slow, excruciating grip like the claw of some demon around the lining of my intestines – probably not much alleviated by the growling on my right – here I am camped out on one of the long benches on the second floor above the check-ins – and sleeping to my side are two relatively homeless looking types: one fat, one thin, both with their hair stuck and flattened out like one big question mark shaped dreadlock, and *de repente* I think I made the wrong decision – I should have sprung for the room.

Dec 30

Another Terrible Idea for a Novel

Chapter 1
D falls for E

Chapter 2
D leaves the country for a very long time

Chapter 3
D returns to the country to find E again

Chapter 4
D casts a spell of black magic to ensure he is able to be with E
and it works – E and D meet and fall in love

Chapter 5
They live happily for a time tearing up the city, let's say it is in
New York until D and E marry

Chapter 6
The wedding, a beautiful disaster on all fronts and precursor
of the misery to come

Chapter 7
The first six months of marriage, E learns to despise D who is now
fatter and poorer – arguments become the central theme of life

Chapter 8
At Christmastime, D has a conversation with E's grandmother,
in which she tells him the story of her own marriage, how

she used to hide under the bed instead of sleep on top of the bed because she was so afraid her husband would accidentally bump her with his knees or elbows during the course of the night, which he was in the habit of doing, injuring her without waking, and that it was after 70 years of marriage, the biggest mistake of her life, she said

Chapter 9, 10, 11, 12, 13, 14, 15, 16, 17, 18, 19, and 20
The story of D and E and their nearly 65 years of marriage

Chapter 21
D dies at age 92

Chapter 22
E, as a widowed grandmother, recounts the story of her life to her grand-daughter and tells her how she met D, fell in love, how he left the country then returned for her years later, how they co-habitated in misery and joy, how they stayed together for nearly 65 years of marriage, how she feels that marrying him was the biggest mistake she ever made and she does not regret a single day.

July 1-2, 2016

Travel day – one of those that must be extended for the sake of preventing further jetlag – otherwise the very smoothest aberration of uncomplicated transit I ever experienced – from the overly cautious, polite and speedy cab ride to Penn Station down Columbus, as I requested and even when it turned to 9th Avenue he asked me if he should continue down 9th Avenue. Was this really happening? He dropped me at 32nd and 7th

Avenue, just at the entryway to NJ Transit, and the escalator took me to a busy line of ticketeers, which I passed, knowing that down the stairs, left in the corridor and to the end of that other hall (where a poem by Kenneth Burke lives, embossed in the lacquered wall, my only companion for many years of waiting for the Newark-bound airport coastline train through Secaucus) – several unattended machines in brilliant orangine readied for my burgeoning one-way off-peak ticket purchase, yet for receipt at $13.00, up 50 cents from the second to last time I rode the NE Corridor line.

Reminder: call granddad to check in about his procedure – "Watchman" operation which sends a net through the vein in his groin and opens up to cover his heart – his heart is now inside this cage.

Once bought, train track 7 appeared on the monitor and like a finely-tuned Swiss tank I lined against the wall ahead of the vast nameless mob and allowed the first three passengers ahead of me, securing an open door held by a conscientious bald black man, and I hushed down the far right side to the front cars and found a seat right away in the senior/handicapped area for my black luggage (XL) and mint-colored (XS) luggage, never smoother or anxiety free each step of the journey thus far, eerily complication-free for New York – the notion that travel in this city could be so devoid of conflict is a never before and probably never again demented experience. Nothing is right today.

On the line at Newark, I went to the front of the online check-in and dropped my bag. Never so hassle-free and was about to get easier. At the security check there was a Greek couple in front of me, and an old guy taking off his shoes, arms over his head through the scanner not recommended for pregnant women or children. There were so few people that a security check which normally takes 45-50 minutes or more was about 3.5 minutes – I even noted to the TSA guard my timing was great this time – she said, yeah, boy you got f-ing miraculous luck.

On the flight itself was my first and only complication, beginning with a half-blind woman in front of me who shoved her eyeball directly two centimeters from the seat listing, and still she had no idea what was represented there by the mysterious Greco-Roman alphanumerical message. In retrospect, she might not have known that seats begin with low numbers and ascend to the higher numbers, because she stopped at #3C,B,A and again at #6F,E,D and again at #7 – you're at #7, I tell her in Portuguese, assuming correctly that she was of Lusitanian descent. When she stops at 10, I tell her you're at 10 and at 12, I ask her, what number is your seat? Thirty-eight, she says, pausing her eyeball on seat #13A. A steward asks to help – tells her the seat is much further on. I am reminded how absurdly slow the culture can be – and I know this makes me a bad anthropologist – mostly it is charming, endearing, idiosyncratic, wonderful, refreshing in its indirectness and anti-logical in its way – how other times, it seems limitlessly unnerving, a grand test of patience unrivaled. For this is one point I adore about the country – delicious procrastinations abound at every corner.

Is there a doctor on board? Please contact the crew.
The #42 seat – with cat – changed to seat #41.
A woman gets up two seats ahead of me and heads towards the front. Then, she turns to the back of the plane, near where the cat was at seat #42. A group of people were huddled around an older woman there who had fainted. I wonder if this was an asthma attack brought on by pets.

July 4, 2016

Vilamoura, Algarve, Portugal

If there is one thing I do not have in this relationship it is independence – there is a kind of spiritual calcification, unfortunately, that pervades my interactions with Eva today. Every exchange is taken as a dispute – to say that I would not like to sit down is just as offensive as if I had spat on her best friend – a nonsensical reaction, it seems, that stems from some general aggression that feels akin to hatred? The other thing I find problematic is when she takes up an argument and her brother also takes up the same, too – but last time I checked the marriage certificate, my wife is listed as "Eva" not as "Eva plus her brother A." But, perhaps next time we have a misunderstanding I can enquire as to the contents of that certificate. Boy, am I an asshole. But really, one never knows what documents really signify. Does it not read that "D" (that's me) is married to "E"? Or does it read that "D" is married to "E" and her brother "A" and her other brother "B"? Or does it read that "D" is married to "E" and her brother "A," her older brother "B," her mother "M" her father "Big A" and E's Grandmother? I admit that I am a fool and do not understand the true significance of marriage. Why am I here?

July 5

Algarve Casino Zombies

All of their faces are crinkled and sucked up, dehydrated like dried pickles in the sun – these gamblers and looters are so pale, their skin having been leeched of all nutrients by the recirculation of an unclean carpet damp with exhausted bile and saturated tobacco smoke with the ground-up bones of pigeons who shit themselves living in the same box unmoving for an eternity – an unspeakable stench that burrows into one's clothing requiring three washes in ultra-hot water and ammonia. The trouble is that the apartment we rented in central Villamoura (its literal translation is Village of the Moors) has intermittent cold-warm-ultrahot water which shuttles unpredictably between ice-cold to boiling hot and back to frigid in a span of 30 seconds – every 30 seconds. Everyone in the family wanted to wash their clothes immediately following the trip to the casino. I won 400 Euros at Roulette playing black – it was necessary however, to dance around the skimmers who were placing hedged bets on groups of numbers – some of the worst of the chronic gamblers were even jumping between two different roulette tables to place bets on two games at once – imagine the same terrible decisions spread across two times over – saying *tem paciência* as if the other players should tolerate their running bets between the wheels. Eva and I always maintained the original 100 Euro bet on black and kept the winnings under my fingers. We backed up at a distance from the frog-eyed pasty creatures hovering around the tables – a few of them were so hideous they might explode the lights with a single terrible gaze. With the winnings on my fourth spin, I took the 100 Euros from the table and cashed out the 500.

It's casual gamblers like us who bankrupt the casinos, said Eva.

I'm sure you're right, I said, because I've only gambled twice in my life, and each time walked away on the up and up.

Dream – everyone is precisely just as ugly on the outside as they are on the inside.

July 6

Revenge of the Towels

Buying a beach towel from a Chinese shop in Algarve is as good as a curse on the family – the towel in our holiday apartment was spotted with black lint like a disgusting slew of bees went there to micturate – for need of a quasi bedsheet, I was forced to buy a towel for 14 Euros which is already extravagant and excessive for a good towel, never mind this overpriced rag. This magnificent towel, when brushed up against any fabric whatsoever leaves behind millions of crappy lint balls which populate and seemingly reproduce and multiply upon every square centimeter of cotton, previously pristine now completely, irreparably sullied – a brand new NY Mets cap, what was just minutes ago a gorgeous imperial blue with a silver embroidered NY – utterly destroyed as if confronted with nuclear fallout – not only lint, but the tiniest of hairs as if I had rubbed up against a mountain lion family picnic. I am returning to the Chinese shop tomorrow and demand my money back or I will stay in their shop and scare the customers until they give me my money – how will I scare the customers? By telling them the truth.

In the morning I was hardly awake (I was in pre-caffeine zombie disarray) when the five of us piled into the car for the marina – then the beach next door. Without coffee I am a mobility-challenged man without a wheelchair – no one could drag me except by the feet – into a productive state of motion. I had an emergency espresso preserved in the fridge, but only remembered it when my zombified toes were filling with sand. I was unable to find even the soles of my feet. Eva, always the grand motivator, pulled at my shorts, exposing me full throttle to a fisherwoman with a rich, gargling voice. She responded to my pecker with animation, and I found the energy for self-transport across the beach. The fisherwoman was perched upon the rocky inlet on the marina's west side awaiting the 8 o'clock torrent of sardines, which flow underneath the inlet diagonal to the shore and out to sea. I managed to forget my indecent exposure, and we swam and took photos, with my brill blue Mets cap and Eva with her cute rainbow cowboy hat, A with his red and black Mets cap I had gifted to him the previous year. At the market was perched red shrimp as big as my head and marzipan in the precise shape of a lob of purple grapes, and bloody fish and fresh sardines, thick cuts of tuna and *carapau*, bread like a yeasty twin.

Eva's father, Big A, had to ask five different locals their version of the quickest route to the market – one, an elderly guy with a polo shirt and belly overtaking his steering wheel, backing his car from one helluva creative parking space which was blocking at least three other cars, who pointed opposite of the sea – westward – and as we edged the lot Big A asked other directions and we took the opposite, towards the sea now – and again along the narrow streets where old ladies were lined up buying *Euro Milhão* lottery tickets at a stale fruit shop – Brazilian avocados, oranges from Florida – which makes no sense as oranges are one of the prized local products and cost one quarter of the price at any market as Big A pointed out – but everything is too convoluted with Eva – the sunscreen which I bought at a 2-for-1 special (even so it was the most expensive sun protection I've ever bought) in which we consulted the pharmacist regarding her allergies and assured us that this was the product best suited for the hypersensitive skin types such as hers – the label on this sunscreen reads "Lait Extreme, tres haute protection sans perfum – sans paraben – peaux photo-sensibles SPF 50" which was supposed to be good for both face and body, but we did not test this claim before leaving Porto for Algarve, thus only in Algarve did she notice that it caused instant redness on her nose, and never used it again. Not only that but as so many things with her allergies, when something causes allergies on her skin, similarly when anyone else wears it she approaches close enough it activates her asthma – which is life-threatening and severely underestimated and misunder-stood – she in other words becomes short on oxygen – making it impossible for me to kiss her or even sit next to her because I am certainly using sunscreen – but this necessitates a shower or series of showers – before entering the bedroom upon arrival from outside. But this type of complication is only a minor, incidental one amongst hundreds of minor, incidental com-plications which seem to arise on a daily basis in my life with Eva. The knife used for butter, for example – if any amount of spicy chorizo, even a single flake were to contaminate the butter, then Big A (who has a digestive condition) may become ill to a serious degree or experience extreme pain because his intestines are simply not built to tolerate spicy foods. These types of aristocratic ailments run in the family – I say aristo-cratic because this is the origin of these diseases – the worst of which is the asthma, regularly sending the family to the emergency room – but before lunch it was my other towel, unfortunately, which enacted its calculated and insidious act upon Eva – when she exited the shower she had forgotten her towel and used mine – which as we had established on day one at the Vilamoura apartment gives her a rash because probably it had been bleached – she reached for it and dried herself but immediately broke out with red splotches – painful as can be, I judged by the wetness and hopelessness in her beautiful eyes as big as the world. Brother A turned on the television later after we had fried sardines, and in America, in Dallas, it had happened again – only this time several police officers were shot with expertise – a message that at this moment, the only sense of social justice for Americans occurs by taking a rifle in one's hands and outright and directly removing authorities from their post by bullet, not by ballet – because as trials for Freddy Gray, Eric Garner, for Trayvon Martin, for Kimani Grey, for so many African-Americian lives are lost without accountability in our American courts, with default acquittals of just about every cop who murdered an innocent life there seems to be no justice of any variety – we live now in the shadow of Michael Brown – who reminds me of Rodney King for the millennial generation – I seem to remember that with Trayvon the jury was made up of all-white folk and one Hispanic woman who was pressured to capitulate, which she did and Zimmerman went free – my guess is that this pattern will continue due to a deeply ingrained system of "old boys" who feed and protect each other's misdeeds from the same basis of white supremacy which bred the kkk – rotten to the marrow, and yet my intuition tells me the worst has yet to reveal its cowardly, acrid face.

July 7

Mystery of the Washing Machine

The washing machine in this apartment in Vilamoura is the bane of clean clothes and simple peace of mind for every person who comes across it.

In the past seventy-two hours, I have had the misfortune of using the machine four times – each time with poorer results, in sessions which vary between four and fourteen hours or more. The washing machine does not stop. It does not respond to human command. It rocks the clothes in murky water for thirty seconds, then pauses, complaining loudly with a hum and a geriatric gargle. The light appears only at the end of the four-hour cycle – but even this is no guarantee – as I learned earlier today that the clothes are ready or finished after the entire afternoon spent spinning and pausing and humming and gargling, the machine came to a moment of finality yet remained in stasis, with the light still on, readying for another pounce on my next false move. Big A has nick-named the machine "Chernobyl" for the fallout of lint that has since besieged my clothes. But what happened with the machine today? Seeing that the light was on, and the machine was seemingly at a point of immobility for several minutes, I opened its door and a flood of water came pouring out onto the kitchen floor. I quickened the hatch back into place but not so emphatically that I would damage the technology. I procured a towel to sop up the mess, but my issue remained unsolved per the clothes, which were now dense with water lodged deep into each fiber of the fabric.

In the evening we went to visit the sea – Eva even saw one of the famous giant red shrimp flitting like the sea cockroach that it is over the shallow ocean floor – having lost its pack, it brushed over her unprepared toes and away from the sun into the Mediterranean. There were too many fathers and daughters playing sea-pong and if one of the balls hit Eva I was prepared to throw it as hard as I could to bury it under the rocks of the inlet. A mediocre saxophonist was puffing over 120 bpm on a six-years prior Top-40 hit, and Eva looked so much more enticing with a ripped t-shirt over her swimsuit than any anorexic lingerie model.

Even so, the haunting image of the Zanussi FLS 522C washing machine remained burned in my brain, with its complex diagram of instructions printed on the front and its cryptic icons and numbers 1 2 3 4 5 6 7 8 9 10 11 12 13, each for a different setting with various combinations of hieroglyphs – this indecipherable language of suds and soaps.

Buying fresh figs at a supermarket – they were sticky and leaking their juices on the tissue paper lining the bottom of the box – we took them for Eva to make jam. She can eat so very few things I am happy if she can consume anything at all, and will always buy.

Returning to the apartment, I asked her mom to assist in the decoding of the washing machine. You can open it, she said, but I explained how I already tried that and the water gushed out. She went with me to the kitchen, where the sly Zanussi lay in wait. There are 13 possible settings, she said, and each setting will cycle through some combination of wash, spin, drain, wash, spin and drain. But apparently, the setting I chose leaves the clothes soaking in water *ad infinitum*. Other settings only spin or only drain water. For this reason, this Spanish-manufactured machine is a completely different animal. She moved it from #11, which had all the symbols in a row, to #6, which contained only the symbol I had interpreted to mean "ocean" and a down arrow. #11, the setting I had chosen, showed a straight line (for water?) and another with dashes inside the water – the meaning of which was lost on me – and another with unmoving water at the bottom. I now understand that the icons should be interpreted in a linear fashion from top to bottom in a long column of glyphs. The end product of setting #11 is that the clothes will sit in a soup of hot water until the customer opens the door, releasing the water into a container for re-use elsewhere. Or else, setting #6 or #13 would drain the water, but it appears that half of these settings result with the clothes sitting, bathing, soaking, basking in liquid bliss. This is the way of the Zanussi washing machine.

Tomorrow, Portugal plays France in the finals of the European football championship.

Atenciòn:

Puerta con aperatura retardada. Una vez finalizado el programa espere 2 a 3 minutos antes de abrir la puerta. Para abrir tire de la manilla suavemente.

The warning written on a sticker placed at the bottom of the machine is written in Spanish only, therefore, I will assume the appliance is of Spanish provenence, and it was purchased for Spanish consumers. Also of note, the selection dial has a repeated number 2, spaced at long and short intervals from the following numbers 2 and 3, respectively.

July 8

The Souvenir Shop

On the way to the marina, in an elevated plaza near the "Champions" bar was not only a tourist shop for souvenirs, but it had the best old postcards, yellowed with time, warped by years sitting in the wire catch – but ceramics too which reminded Eva of the famous Bordallo Pinheiro ceramics – copies, if well made imitations of the famous ceramicists' cabbage plates with two mice, long tails curling across the rim. The shopkeeper pulled out the postcard rack into the middle of the crowded aisle so we could turn it, then proceeded to tell Eva's brother A about his diabetes, his wife's heart disease, and his amputated toe, all while Eva fingered the reproductions of Pinheiro's pigs heads, sardine-shaped searing plates, and tomato-top sauce containers, all six Euros apiece. Take one, I said, I'll buy it for you. We can always come back tomorrow, said Eva, but it seemed the shopkeeper spoke more quickly then.

We bought only 4 postcards. One of the postcards showed a family on a horse and buggy with straight-brimmed hats, all black, scarves tied under their necks, smiling in the sun, perched over the wooden wheels of the cart. There was a spot over the horse's mane in the photograph that was sun-faded, like it had been facing the window unmoving, summer after summer for twenty years.

The next day we returned to the shop at 2:30pm, and read that the sign said open at 3 — so we got a mineral water at "Champions" and waited outside the bar there, while the bartender watched some preliminary football championship warm-ups. We were waiting, and Eva's brother A joined us, anticipating further purchases. By now, Eva had decided she wanted at least the olive dish — shaped as a branch of the olive tree — and the orange salt and pepper — shaped as an orange fruit. But at 3:10, with still no sign of the shopkeeper, I walked through the blistering sun across the plaza to see about the store. Although we could see the window and the front door from our vantage at the bar, when I got to the door I was not surprised to see it was still closed, as it appeared from "Champions." The shopkeeper was missing and so was his diabetes. The lights were off inside, the shutters were down, the dust getting thicker.

Told you, said Eva, when I returned to the table.

Told me what?

That it would be closed, Eva said.

We stayed at "Champions" until 4pm, when we were joined by Eva's brother B, who also had heard about the place and wanted to see the store. But it was simply not to be on that day. B wanted to stroll the marina, and score a hand-made ice cream of the sort they remember eating as kids first visiting the Algarve. It was nearly 4:30 when we walked to the streetside facade to see if somehow the shopkeeper had returned to the other entrance, but the shop and all of its contents remained out of reach.

Returning to the apartment around 6, sated with sugared lips from the cold cream, we could see from the main walkway – still beat down by the sun at a lesser angle of brutality – that the man would not appear until long after *siesta*, if he reappeared at all.

We resolved to return soon.

The next day, the city was filled with dogs – the one by the grocery store with all his hair shaved except a toupee at the top of his brow – three curly hairs remained there – the hairs appeared like the joke of a joke – over foggy eyes this dog had no awareness of just how unseemly it had become, sculpted in all the wrong directions.

We waited to try one more time for the 6-euro cabbage ceramics, for the clay rodents that garnish the plates. Also, the bar across the plaza was the only place in Vilamoura that served espresso at the normal, non-tourist price of 0.65 Euro, but was always stained with coffee grounds on the lip of the cup.

Between "Champions" and the apartment there were two ways to reach the plaza where the coveted souvenir shop was – either the main road, polluted by heavy traffic and a gas station – or a back pathway strewn with purple buds and pedals of a now cultivated wildflower, leading to the post office and then across to the plaza. We took the flower path this time and were immediately under siege – heavily allergic to dogs, Eva and I hollered at the owners when their canines circled us: pugs, boxers, terriers, dobermans, there were all manner and breed of dogs without leash and they were all attracted to me and Eva – like the other night at the marina when Pekinese after Pekinese tormented us at the fishy docks, and then we saw a large blue duffle bag, unattended while we waited for a table (dinner date with an old friend of the family). There were tourist shops, two in a row at the corner of the dock where sat the bag, and Eva looked at me with a questioning eye. The crowd was thick and dozens had already passed over the pack – but it remained unclaimed. I started to get nervous, having read too many newspapers and worked in journalism myself, I suspected the worst was about to happen, and Eva agreed it was a disconcerting scenario. There was a security guard, and we got his attention. He leaned over to speak with us, and a tall Norwegian type at that moment picked up the duffle bag and moseyed.

But on the flowered path, we escaped the wrath of the puppies, and found our souvenir shop closed.

Is there some kind of national holiday? I asked Eva.

No, not that I know of.

Is there a local or regional holiday of some kind?

I don't think so, she said. Let's come back tonight to see if he's around.

We made it to the mini-golf course. Eva beat me in 18 holes easily, but I had known it already by the time we reached the dinosaur with a broken tail at hole 8. She beat me and I could not pretend that I had let her – she was simply better. Afterwards, we skipped the smelly arcade room, returned the golf clubs and emerged again on the overpollinated walkway.

Again, the souvenir shop was closed. It was 6pm, and we stopped at "Champions" for a coffee. They brought me their reliable espresso shot with a few grounds drizzled atop the edge of the cup. We waited until 7:30pm, and still no shopkeeper. Still no ceramic cabbage.

We had one more day in Algarve. We woke up late to the sound of the city driving fast and honking. People were hollering. Portugal had just won their first ever Eurocup championship in France, against the home team no less. The only possibility was that madness would follow.

Needless as it may be to state, the souvenir shop was closed, and we left Algarve the following day, with yet another mystery unsolved.

Don't forget: *ponte* = bridge

but

ponta = penis

and

piscina = swimming pool

but

pichinha = penis (diminutive)

Made two more slips of the Freudian variety on this trip – the first was when after a morning trip to the *Lota* – fresh fish market – when Big A haggled between vendors for the best *petinga* – baby sardines, which are illegal.

They must not have bloodshot eyes, he said and if they do it means you leave them dead in the market. Those were not caught today. The slip I made went like this: I was trying to say that I had never been to this *mercado*, but only the *mercado de Matosinhos*, which is located, as I attempted to say, close to the bridge – but instead I said it was the market close to the penis (*ponta*).

There are a few details of this trip to Vilamoura I have forgotten to note:

1. The path we meandered to the beach on day one was via the main road, which leads us to walk on the highway itself, as there is no sidewalk between the few yards from the apartment to the gas station.

2. There is a back way, a pedestrian path, half a street down, which is filled with gardenias, philodendrons and tall reaching flowers which nearly block the path with their lingering pods – leading to the side entrance of the post office – a very modest stucco building built with a Moorish flourish – it was Vilamoura after all – village of the Moors.

3. The swimming pool, nestled with the apartment complex – upon first consideration I thought it to be blue with chlorine – but later deducted it was colored from the tiles, many of which were chipped or broken entirely, as Eva discovered when first entering the pool – but I never stepped on one – not even one of the broken tiles.

There were two main events to note about the pool – the first was that I was locked out of the apartment without a key after an argument with Eva. The argument had to do with my performing calisthenics spontaneously outside the door of the rented apartment. My elbow swinging was somehow offensive to her – an aristocratic notion that certain motions were more dignified than others? I may never know. But in the swimming pool I was sun-soaking solo, unable to return to the building – trapped both metaphorically and realistically, but not trapped inside a room – as confined in a cell, for example – but simply limited in choice and ability to independently exit the swimming courtyard. I noticed Eva's mother in their kitchen window and tried signaling to her, but she would not meet my gaze, or if she did, nothing came of it. The door to the re-entry was locked, and so I asked a guy to borrow his keys but he only had a key to a connected building, which led to the neighboring halls of the wrong side of the apartment complex – I had to return to the pool area again until another walked from the central building, and he led me through after I interrupted his conversation with his companion.

The other incident was the tipoff that chlorine levels were dangerously low if existent at all in the pool – three large seagulls who had been circling overhead had landed poolside and dunked their beaks in the water. The largest of them started up and flapped his way directly into the water in the very center, scaring an old woman who was whaling over a beach ball. Then, one more seagull did a nosedive from a perch at the top of the central apartment wall, as if lobbing after live fish for the kill.

The next morning, these same seagulls were bathing their feathers and tumbling in the kiddie pool. A mosquito bigger than a dragonfly raced through the middle like a speedboat.

After these observations, we never touched the water.

But being trapped in the swimming area I was faced with the idea that

I should contemplate the ways in which I had trapped myself – nobody had forced me to go into the pool area, and I knew that a key was needed to re-enter – relying on the usual, that someone props the door of re-entry with a folded over carpet in the lobby – thus I intentionally had myself locked into that situation – which was almost terrifying but even then I recognized the comedy. I am my very own totalitarian regime, ruling over only one subject – myself. I oppress myself, I contain multitudes of ways to oppress myself – hear my barbaric yelp of self-imposed incarceration as I cage myself in a chlorine-less pool where seagulls leave traces of who knows what diseases. I am the world's most efficient self-perpetuating panopticon, a deadly weapon programmed for use against just one human being – I am both serf and king, slave and master, dictator and dictated.

After 40 minutes of Dvorzak allegros E stuck her finger into my nostrils

What's the difference between a jerk person, a kneejerk, and beef jerky? Eva says. And what about jerking off?

July 10

Towel of Champions, Revisited

Now I am sleeping on the back porch of the apartment in Villamoura, my legs horizontal only by virtue of two plastic lawn chairs.

There is good reason for this. Eva is convinced that – after finding a single strand of red hair matching the Chinese towel – the towel has contaminated and inhabited my body inextricably, such that only after several days of backstroking and wading through salt water will I shake the fibers from my follicles, nails, orifices, wrinkles. Thus, I am constricted to a 48-hour period of quarantine on the veranda.

Again, I have proven an impressive expertise for self-damnation. I awaken with the sun, my forehead already blistered from the UV rays. I slide open the glass door into the kitchen, slip an espresso pod into the machine and wait. I have placed the pod in upside down. The warm brown water dregs will have to suffice, now, as my legs remain forever cramped up from the wasted position on two plastic lawn chairs.

As my eyes flutter with the last bits of sleep, I notice a reddish sliver caught in the hairs on the back of my middle knuckle – apparently Eva was correct. A breeze slips in through the sliding door, picks up the reddish strand and delivers it stuck to the door of the washing machine.

Preface #91

Leaving Las Vegas

This is a story about a man who tries to drink himself to death with water.

In the first scene, the man is shopping, swooning through the isles of a grocery store picking out varieties of natural mineral water, carbonated water, seltzer water, distilled water, spring water from all manner of spring, going absolutely bonkers with bottles and glasses of water, gallons of water, liters and milliliters of water. When he arrives to his hotel room, he opens the tap and plunges his head recklessly underneath the faucet, gurgling and spraying the H20 all across the walls. The man is unhinged, the hotel room a chaos of strewn water containers. He straps on his running shoes, rips off all his other clothes, enters the bathtub. He runs the faucet, submerges himself naked in his shoes, mouth agape in the steaming liquid. He loses consciousness. He awakens to the sound of the hotel alarm clock, jumps out of the bath and attempts to drink an entire gallon of water but stops short, vomiting clear liquid onto the floor. He pounds his fists on the floor, he howls – now in tears, he crawls to his suitcase, unzips the hard case, fishes around for baby bottle and a bib, places the bib around his neck, puts the baby bottle to his lips, crawls into fetal position sucking on the baby bottle. There is a knock on the door.

Delivery, says the bellhop, as he brings in dolly after dolly of giant water coolers. Just stack it over there, says the crazy man, not moving from his fetal posture.

Doggie at the MAAT

We are back in Porto after our Algarve trip. Last night, as we had dinner with guests just in from Lisbon, and Big A surprised me with a rather odd tale from a contemporary museum in Lisbon:

There was one of those skintight creatures that fits in a woman's purse, only this one decided it wanted to accompany its master into the MAAT Museum on all fours, and this wiener liked the garbage can sculpture in the middle of the room so well that it took a real-life dump there, perhaps to lend the installation the authenticity it deserved. The dog shimmied, backed up to the sculpture, and winked, and out came a warm steamer right there on the white marble. The breezy owner walked away with the beast, and continued through the next room – innocently looking at the paintings, popping in and out of curtains and viewing the videos as if nothing at all had happened. In keeping with this narrative of nonchalance, none of the other museum-goers said anything about the dog's act, and a few of them took this to be part of a performance. This perception was evidenced by a man dressed in a tweed sports coat who asked the pet-owner a question: what kind of reception have you had at other museums? To which the kind lady replied, I have never been to a museum before. With that, she walked out the door, but not without leaving behind a few footprints of burnt sienna.

Next, the cleaning lady came along to see about the mess. I know exactly what to do, she says, and returns a few minutes later with a handful of paper towels. She spreads the paper towels across the center of the room, covering not only the place of defecation, but a wide range around it. Then, she begins to dance. She places one foot on top of the paper towels, smashing the warm, mushy fecal matter underneath – then many more gleeful steps around it, like a meringue marmalade of poo-poo. Surely, the more she dances the cleaner the floor will be. As she does this, she hums a sweet tune.

Along comes one of the curators of the museum.

Mariana, what are you doing?

Oh, you'll see. The place will be good as new, says Mariana, still dancing.

Mariana picks up the paper towels with a confident air, sweeping most of the chunks left behind by the pooch, but there is a long, thin smear still extant as she piles the paper. She takes another paper, places it over the smear, stomps on top of it with her boots like a five-year old child throwing a tantrum. When she finishes, the paper towels have absorbed the chunkiness but left a deep yellow-tinted, banana-shaped stain on the tiles.

Well, says Mariana, artists' work comes and goes, but we will always remember that doggie's contribution to the museum. Mariana walks away, the fecal smear still quite present and bold on the marble.

Publisher at the Beach

Eva and I were sitting having a coffee, as was not unusual, on the deck by the beach at a place called Marspresso. When I say coffee, I mean a shot of quality espresso, never bitter – the way most American baristas make it – and filled up all the way to the top of the cup, *cheiu*. When I say the beach I mean we could hear, see and smell the surf from that wooden deck, and if we stepped off we would be walking in the sand. We were there several times per week doing just this, enjoying each other's company and the ocean.

What happened on this particular day was that I was approached by a publisher while we were drinking our espressos. But this term, publisher, should be understood in a very loose sense, even in a reckless sense. This was a person – as she herself explained – who approached people randomly at the beach to see if she could sell the books that she published. She carried these books with her, in her hands. There were three books. All three had the word *poetry* in the title or the subtitle, each with a different color cover and white pages in between, each written by the same author with his same author photo on the back sleeve.

You can hold them if you like, she said. You can read them. They're real.

Are your books available in bookstores? I asked.

No, she said, I prefer to market at the beach.

That's an interesting approach, said Eva. Why?

For me, I like to walk along the beach, I like to smell the ocean, and sell the books in person – one reader at a time. Go ahead, page through the book, says the publisher. The book is made up of real pages.

Are these books available online? Eva said.

No.

Do you have plans to expand the number of authors?

No, we like this author.

I don't really like to read poetry, Eva said.

St. Merde and the Puke Dancer

First, there was the billboard. The billboard was based on a painting or maybe it was a print of the painting. The painting featured a saint, with a halo, and a dress, and sandals. The billboard was advertising a festival in honor of *St. Mamede*, which I pronounced out loud St. Ma-Merde, according to Eva. I personally tend to think she hears a different type of "r" than I do, and it appears to her that I had placed an "r" sound in the word Mamede. That was not my intention. Later that night, when darkness was around us and we had wrestled our way into the crowd at the so-named Beach Party, located just across the highway from the blinking lights and towers of the enormous grounds – practically a city in itself – which houses the petrol refinery. The refinery had some recent near-accidents, in which the entire section of town was on the verge of exploding. This is no exaggeration, as the area consists of millions of liters of gasoline which would, in a chain reaction, light the north of Porto aflame in a matter of seconds. Therefore, this blast radius was the ideal location for a gathering of thousands of completely obliterated and belligerent teenagers who, due to a shortage of outhouses would crawl across the highway – inebriated and without diapers – to micturate on the fence of the petrol yard. The Beach Party was swarmed with kids, balloons of crowds loosely ushered into the entrance gate, of which the organizers only had one, and (probably illegal) only had one narrow point of exit. Safety oversight does not seem to be a point of strength in Portugal.

After the pat down search, we entered the grounds and proceeded to make out like 16 year-olds. To our left, there was a cameraman with unsecured tripod whose lens was trained on the laser light show onstage. He abandoned his post and a gnarly wind came up and swirled the tarp over his camera. Down came the camera. Soon, the smoke machines and sub-woofer grew louder, and the crowd filled in. Girls appeared around the necks of their broad-shouldered boyfriends. One of these girls was shaken from the hoist up, apparently, and vomited over her boyfriends' shoulder. Someone's backpack got hit by the sludge, and someone else's tennis shoes. Then they started to kiss a sexy, post-vomit kiss. The girl was wearing cutoff jean shorts and a short blouse stuck above her waistline, and as she reached around for the tongue, her crack was exposed. A jaunty passerby took this opportunity to probe a finger there, then put this same finger into his mouth. The lights from the stage pushed a green luminescence out and over the people with long, smoky geometry.

Another No-No

Eva was playing the candy game on my tablet. Now I have to compete with that thing for her attention. She can play while I write – but last night, I said another no-no.

Apparently, I continue to have an impeccable knack for saying something very sexual in Portuguese. I thought she won a prize, because she exclaimed *Ah! Queijinho!*

Naturally, I was curious what this prize was, as I only assumed that it meant that it was a smallish block of cheese, due to its suffix over the root word meaning cheese being diminutive. Show me the cheese, then, I wanted to say, and so logically, I formulated my translation: *mostra queijinho,* which of course means show me your ass.

Eva then felt compelled to share this information with her mother, this amusing nugget of my most recent linguistic faux-pas. Eva's mother turned around and faked pulling down her pants.

Eva's Nightmare

A guy puts a finger inside his own hole, then runs around with the finger stained with poo, trying to put his finger into everyone's hole.

Her grandmother – who of course has to be present for this spectacle – sighs and says, Young people, these days.

More Room

Again as we were sleeping last night, Eva pushes me over against the wall so that my left side is pressed up onto the cold stone.

Give me more room or you leave, she says.

My arms are straight at my sides. My legs are taut.

I need more room, she says, her elbow weighing on the back of my hand.

I slide across the bottom of the mattress, careful not to trip her knees. I go downstairs, open my suitcase, fish around for a pair of boxers and a t-shirt and remove to the bathroom to change. I drink two cups coffee, eat bread and butter. It is five am. I continue where I left off in an abominable, perplexing English translation of *Love Sonnets*, by Camões:

> a furry thing with no name
> a vengeful and silent release...

I retreat to the livingroom sofa, and curl up there without blanket trying to doze. Lightening strikes so close it sounds as if on the sidewalk in front of the house. My legs go numb from circulation cut off on the blunt edge of the loveseat, the cushions long since defeated. More thunder rumbles.

At 9 am, the cleaning lady appears. At 10 am, the postman knocks, delivering a package wrapped in yellow tape for Eva's brother A. My body feels like it has been tumbled in a washing machine and then blow-dried. At 11 am, the neighbor lady delivers turnips from her sister's farm. At 12pm, Eva's brother A wakes up, retrieves the package from the stairs, and goes back to sleep. The cleaning lady opens an umbrella at the front door, balances on her new high heels, and leaves. Thunder strikes once more. I lace up my Italian tennis shoes and go for a jog to the lighthouse and back, completely wet from the drizzle. At 2pm, Eva's brother is awake, poking a crispy chicken in the oven.

I'm pregnant, says Eva, descending the stairs in a *Kiss* t-shirt and panties. But the word is much better in Portuguese: *grávida*. It makes me think of *gravitas,* derived from the Latin *gravis,* meaning serious.

Late July, 2016

It's a damn cliché but it's the overbearing truth – every time I think about returning to NY from Portugal, America seems more bitter, more resigned to constant violence, more racially fractured and hateful – just before my trip I was jaywalking down third Avenue, jocked up for a souvenir rampage when a girl stopped at a corner and was viciously groped by a speedy, jaggedly moving dude with a lop-sided gait and frayed denim jeans. Not that there aren't predatorial creeps in Porto – I know for a fact they exist in the land of giant shrimp as well. But after Dallas, after Baton Rouge, after Baltimore was denied justice once again, I feel that we are in the midst of another necessary, albeit brutal civil rights era – civil rights part II – more than 50 years after MLK.

Grandmother's Tales

Last Sunday, Eva's grandmother had come around for lunch-time, as per the usual family schedule. In the kitchen, she re-counted stories of the family, beginning with her daughter, Eva's Aunt C.

My daughter, she said, was so gorgeous when she was young that every day men attacked her with kisses. She was a rare blond with blue eyes, a striking natural blond so un-common in Portugal the men saw her as exotic, and they would mob her at every turn – riding the elevator in Ribeira for example, down to the river level – I remember when she stepped out of the elevator and she was standing next to a man whose hair was in a state of chaos, and he was bleeding all over his forehead and cheeks, with cuts everywhere along his neck like he was mauled by a cat — and I asked, what happened? Nothing, said Aunt C. The guy straightened his tie, patted down his hair and walked away quickly. Only later she told me that the "gentleman" had tried to kiss her, and she had said no, but he did not stop. The elevator was a long ride, and it was just the two of them so she clawed at his face with her nails until he stopped. Another time, at the doctor's office — and here grandmother emphasized the word doctor — that this was not the only instance this had happened at the doctor's office — Aunt C was called into the examination room, and within seconds Aunt C could be heard shrieking and there was a loud crashing sound, then Aunt C emerged — Let's go, she said. Again I asked her what happened? Nothing, she said. As we were driving to another doctor's office, she told me how the doctor accosted her with kisses and she slapped him three, four, five times in a row. The doctor stumbled back against a cabinet and the cabinet fell, making a crashing sound.

In Spain, we were in Madrid — what did the men do in Madrid when they saw her? They went absolutely mad — she was followed in the streets every moment, she was always slapping men and hitting them with her purse but hitting them hard in the face. It was no joke — she was pursued on a daily basis. But Madrid was horrible. We went to a place during the daytime — it was the middle of the afternoon, and we had been visiting the Prado — we were having a teatime break at a bakery nearby — I think we were only there for twenty minutes, but there must have been fifteen men that just came to our table to see her — men from the neighborhood who had heard about her, the famous blond — she looked like a movie star to them — a man would sit next to her and he would try to kiss her and she would slap him, and he would go away. Then another man would sit down next to her and try the same thing. It was like a roulette wheel of men, one after another, each trying to kiss her, each of them slapped and departed. Her hand was so sore from slapping the men she started using her left. She got pretty good with that left. We walked away from that bakery and guess what? There was another one who followed us on the street. They were like dogs after her scent, these men.

My brother, grandma said, was a very tough and a very strong man, but he was an honorable man. He was a soldier, and he fought in the war. One day he was wandering the neighborhood – he had many friends and they were out for a stroll. They were talking philosophy – he loved philosophy – they were debating Nietzsche or Schopenhauer, I don't remember which one it was – when they came upon these kids playing soccer in the street. The soccer ball flew out of control, and maybe it hit a policeman or maybe the policeman was just in a rotten mood. The policeman approached one of the boys and started beating him over the head – a young boy about 9 years old – and he wouldn't stop. What did my brother do? He shook the policeman and slapped him with both sides of his hand, removed his hat and flung it across to the dumpster, slapped him more and unbuttoned his uniform. He removed the pants. He scattered the guy's uniform all over the neighborhood – he left the guy dazed, wearing only a pair of briefs.

About the Author

David Moscovich is the Romanian-American author of *You Are Make Very Important Bathtime* (JEF Books, 2013) and *LIFE+70[Redacted]*, a print version of the single most expensive literary e-book to ever be hacked (Lit Fest Press, 2016.) *Blink If You Love Me* is his latest novel, published by Adelaide Books.

You Are Make Very Important Bathtime (JEF Books: Chicago, 2013) is a novel of flash fictions about a Westerner's failure to navigate Japanese culture clash, a celebration of the beauty of misunderstanding and the inadvertent poetry of bad grammar. *LIFE+70 [Redacted]*, published by Lit Fest Press in 2016, is the printed version of the single most expensive literary e-book ever to be hacked. Before it was stolen, the one and only e-book was priced at US$249,999.99.

Moscovich's *Blink If You Love Me* (Adelaide Books, 2019), set in modern-day Portugal, is a novel about the intimacies and cultural, socio-linguistic idiosyncrasies inherent in marrying into and cohabiting with a close-knit family as an outsider. Struggling with his adopted tongue, the narrator of the novel is cursed with a tendency to imbue everyday speech with innuendo at large family gatherings. His wife Eva's unique perspective and approach to coping proves to be transformative, as the newlyweds adapt to their ridiculously disharmonious lifestyle.

Recipient of fellowships from New York University, International House New York and sponsorship from the New York Foundation for the Arts (NYFA), he holds an MFA in Fiction from NYU and is editor and publisher of Louffa Press, a micro-press dedicated to printing innovative fiction in collectible, handprinted chapbooks as well as artist books.

Moscovich is a writer and freelance journalist and lives in New York City and Porto, Portugal.